It's a Wonderful Werewolf

New York Times and **USA Today** Bestselling Author

CYNTHIA EDEN

CHAPTER ONE

The attack came from out of nowhere. One moment, Oliver Abbott was bending down on one knee and pulling out the diamond ring that he'd so carefully chosen for Gia Donato. His hands weren't shaking from the cold. They were shaking because for the first time in his life, Oliver was truly terrified.

This was it. His big moment. He wanted to spend the rest of his life with Gia. His mouth opened to deliver the proposal that he'd oh-so-carefully rehearsed.

And then...

He was hit from behind. Something powerful and hard slammed into him even as Gia screamed. The diamond ring flew from Oliver's fingers and hit the white snow...only, all of the snow wasn't white. It was...red.

Blood?

"*Oliver!*" Gia's frantic voice.

He managed to twist, and he shoved off his attacker. But it wasn't a person who'd attacked him. It was the biggest, ugliest dog he'd ever seen in his life. Blood dripped from the creature's razor-sharp fangs, and its bright, glittering eyes were locked on Oliver with what appeared to be absolute hate.

"A wolf," Gia whispered. "Oh, God, Oliver, you were *bitten—*"

He could feel that. He knew his blood was dripping into the snow.

At her voice, the wolf's attention—a wolf, not a dog, a freaking *wolf*—swung toward her. The animal let out a low and lethal growl, and its powerful body leaned low to the ground. Oliver knew it was going to lunge and attack her even before the wolf sprang forward.

So when it *did* leap for her, Oliver was in its path. He put his body before Gia even as she screamed in horror. The wolf barreled into him. Its mouth tore into Oliver's shoulder and neck. He could have sworn that the asshole beast *laughed* as its teeth gouged Oliver. *Sonofabitch.* The bite *hurt.* Hurt even more than the bullets he'd taken while on overseas missions with his SEAL team.

Oliver shoved his hand into his pocket and grabbed for the old pocketknife that he always kept close. The thing was a certifiable antique, and his grandfather had sworn it had been giving his family good luck for generations.

Even as the growls of the beast filled his ears and even as his blood poured down his body,

Oliver yanked out the treasured knife. He saw Gia run behind the beast and grab its tail.

"Get off him!" she yelled.

The wolf lifted its head and turned toward her to bite—

Oliver shoved his knife into the beast. For an instant, Oliver could have sworn that he smelled something burning. That some smoke even rose into the air...

The wolf let out a loud, keening howl as it jerked from Oliver. It turned and rushed away, leaving a trail of blood in the snow.

And taking Oliver's knife as the beast fled...because the knife had still been embedded in the wolf's chest.

For a moment, Oliver stared numbly after the animal. His mind struggled to process exactly what had just happened.

Attacked. Attacked by an actual wolf. Sure, everyone knew there were wolves out in the wild near Jasper, Colorado, but wolves didn't come into town and randomly *bite* people. That shit just did not happen as a general rule.

"Oh, God, that's so much blood." Gia jumped for him.

Too late. His legs had given out on him, and Oliver hit the snow-covered ground. His body felt funny. Not cold, but red-hot. Burning hot. He was suddenly shaking everywhere. Hard tremors that jolted his body.

"What's happening?" Gia's hands clamped around him. "Are you having a seizure?"

Oliver didn't know that the hell he was having. He stared straight up and saw the full moon above him.

"It's going to be all right," Gia promised.

He was getting even hotter. The tips of his fingers felt weird. Like…like his damn fingernails were breaking off. And why were his teeth hurting?

"I'm calling an ambulance! He bit you, but you're going to be fine!"

Maybe he needed some serious rabies shots. Maybe he needed—

His bones were popping. Oliver shouted out in pain as his body contorted.

Okay, that wasn't fucking normal. He knew that. This reaction wasn't due to rabies. This was…*what the hell is this?*

"Oliver?" Gia's desperate voice.

Oliver dragged his gaze off the beautiful, mesmerizing moon. Made himself look at her. But when his head turned toward her…

He heard a heavy thumping. Too fast. Too hard. Too tempting. His gaze zeroed in on her neck where her pulse raced, and he thought…

It would be so easy to rip open her throat.

Oliver's breath sawed out. What the hell? What was he thinking? He *loved* Gia. Loved her more than his life. He would never, ever want to so much as bruise her, much less rip out her throat!

And why was he hurting so damn badly?

Oliver tried to lift up his hand so he could touch the wounds on his neck and shoulder, and he heard Gia's sharp gasp.

"Oliver..." Terrified. Shocked.

He looked at his hand. Except his fingers looked funny. Long, black *claws* had sprung from the fingertips. "N-no—" But that wasn't what emerged from his mouth. Only a growl came out. Animalistic.

Then white-hot fire poured through his whole body, and he *howled* at the pain. Howled and jumped to his feet, only to stumble forward and immediately slam down on all fours.

"Let me help you!" Gia was almost begging.

But he was staring down at his claws, and he was seeing that his fingers were shifting into something else—something that looked like paws. Either he was having the craziest hallucination of his life or—

Or I'm turning into a wolf.

Another wave of that agonizing pain hit him. Gia grabbed for him, and her sweet scent wrapped around him. The sound of her racing heart filled his ears, and once more, a terrible temptation grew in him.

So easy to bite...

"Get away!" Oliver attempted to shout at her. But no words came. Only snarls and growls.

Instinct took over. The trail of blood that the wolf had left was in front of him. A trail that led out of the park and into the dark woods. He bounded forward and followed that trail even as Gia shouted his name behind him.

And when the woods surrounded Oliver, when he was far, far away from Gia, then the change took him completely.

***

Gia held the engagement ring in her palm. A blood-soaked diamond ring. "Please, Officer," Gia said to the cop who stood before her. "You have to help me find my boyfriend." She pointed to the trail of blood. She'd rushed after him, but he'd been moving so fast, and, as incredible as it seemed, Gia was pretty sure that Oliver had been running on all fours as he fled.

Like a wolf.

And he had a wolf's claws.

But she didn't say that. Couldn't say any of that because the nice cop would think she was stark-raving crazy. "He was bitten and he's bleeding, and he needs to be in a hospital!"

The cop gave her a reassuring nod. "Don't you worry. We will find him. I'll get more officers out here to help me search."

But she *was* worrying. The snow was falling again, and the chill in the air was just getting worse and worse. Oliver was out there, all alone and hurt. She'd lost him in the woods, and she was so afraid something terrible was happening to him.

A long, low howl cut through the night.

***

"Miss? Miss, you need to go home."

Gia was chilled to the bone. Her teeth wouldn't stop chattering. "I can't. We haven't found Oliver." They'd searched for hours. Brought in spotlights. Brought in the best tracking canines in the county, but the dogs had barely stepped foot into the dark woods around the park before they'd immediately turned and run back out, yelping.

"We will keep searching, but you need to get home." The officer was compassionate but determined. "What if he's there? What if he's at your house? What if your friend walked there during the night?"

The night was over. The sun was starting to slip over the horizon. She could just see the faint, golden edges of light trickling through the trees. "He's not there. Not at my place. Not at his. I called and had neighbors check at both locations." Resolution straightened her weary shoulders. "He's out in the woods, and I'm not leaving until—"

Oliver was walking toward her. Completely naked as he came out of the wilderness. His steps were a little slow. His body uncertain. Gia let out a shrill cry of relief and rushed toward him. She wrapped him tightly in her arms. He was okay! He was...

Burning hot.

Her body shuddered against his. She lifted her head. Stared into his eyes. "I was so scared!" Her words tumbled out. "We searched and searched, and you weren't anywhere! You—"

"Let me go."

His voice was off. Too flat.

Gia slowly released him. Her gaze swept over him as more worry twisted through her, and she realized—he had no wounds. No cuts. No bites. Nothing. He was completely naked in front of her and there was no sign that he'd ever been injured even though she'd *seen* the wolf bite him.

She jerked out of her coat. Handed it to him. "You—you need to cover up." A glance to the side showed the cops were closing in on them. "Listen to me." Her voice was urgent. "Everything is going to be *fine*."

But Oliver shook his head. "No, sweetheart, it's not."

Chapter Two

"The answer is yes." Gia walked slowly into the den. He heard every soft rustle of her steps.

Oliver stood at the fireplace, his forearm propped on the mantel, and his gaze resting on the fire that twisted and danced. As she approached him, he stiffened slightly, his powerful shoulders tensing as her light, vanilla scent swept around him. A flare of hunger, white-hot lust, burned in him, but he choked it down. Then, slowly, making sure he'd schooled his expression, Oliver glanced back at her. "I don't remember asking a question."

"You asked a question two nights ago." Her dark hair slid over her shoulders. God, she was gorgeous. All smooth, honey skin, deep, dark eyes, and plump, red lips. She looked good enough to gobble up.

Yeah, you are not doing that shit. Slowly, he turned to fully face her.

Gia opened her hand to show the ring that nestled in her palm. "My answer is yes."

A muscle flexed along his jaw as he looked at the ring. He'd thought it had been lost in the snow, but Gia must have found it. Kept it. The silence stretched between them. A silence that was way, way too long and uncomfortable.

His gaze lifted to her face. Her delicate jaw hardened as she took the ring and shoved it on her finger.

"Gia..."

She rushed toward him. Put her hands on his chest. Her touch scorched him. "Nothing has changed. I love you. You love me." Her gaze searched his. "Let's go forward. Everything can be—"

"We both know I'm not fine." He cut through her words because the last thing he wanted to hear from her was a lie. *Everything cannot be fine. We can't go forward. There is no going forward from this hell.*

Her lips pressed together. He caught the flash of pain on her face before she whispered, "It was one night."

One horrible, terrifying night.

"Only one night, Oliver. It doesn't have to be the end!"

Yes, it did. "I fucking became a wolf, Gia." A damn werewolf. He hadn't told that story to the cops. If he had, they would have thought he was insane. They would have locked him away. Hell, *he* thought it was crazy. Utter madness.

Except...

Except he remembered his bones popping and reshaping. He remembered fur exploding over his body. He remembered running over the snow and being able to hear every single sound in those woods. He'd easily evaded the cops—and Gia—because he'd known exactly where they were even when he'd been miles away from their location. He'd stayed as a wolf until the sun rose, and then the transformation back into the form of a man had been just as brutal as the first shift.

But, when it had ended, his wounds from the initial attack had been gone. There hadn't even been a scratch on him.

Now, her hands were on him. She was pressing hard to his chest, and he could only shake his head. "How can you even touch me?"

"Stop it!" An angry reprimand from her. "I can touch you because it's *you*. So you got furry, so what?"

Got furry?

"And you had claws—yes, I saw those by the way. I also caught a glimpse of your paws when you hit down on all fours, right before you rushed into the woods. I saw it all, and I do not care." Her dark gaze didn't waver. "It's still *you*."

But it wasn't. He wasn't the same man he'd been before the attack. The wolf had bitten him, and Oliver had changed.

He'd seen some scary shit in his time. While he'd been a Navy SEAL, he'd gone into some dark places—physically and mentally. He knew the world was full of danger, but he'd never, ever expected to find out that monsters—*actual monsters*, not just shitty humans—were real.

Yet now, he was one of those monsters. "It's not safe for you to be around me."

Her eyes widened. Then she *laughed*. As if Oliver had just told her the funniest joke ever. Since she'd often teased him about being too serious—she was the more light-hearted one—he knew he hadn't said a damn funny thing.

But she laughed until tears filled her eyes. "No way." She swiped a hand over her cheek. "You would never hurt me."

He wouldn't. But... "The wolf might."

She swallowed and stepped back. Gia wasn't touching him at all any longer, and he missed her touch. He'd fallen hard and fast for her the first day they'd met. They'd been at a Christmas tree lot. He'd gone reluctantly because he'd figured he should do something to brighten up his place. When he'd walked past the festively decorated entrance, he'd collided with a seven-foot fir...a fir that had been precariously clutched by Gia.

The tree had toppled, so had she—and so had Oliver. So, yes, he'd *literally* fallen hard and fast for her.

Then he'd offered her hot chocolate, and she'd given him her slow, gorgeous grin. The grin that made her single dimple—in her left cheek—wink.

The dimple wasn't winking now. A little furrow was between her brows. Her "thinking" face. Whenever she slipped into her deep concentration mode, the furrow would appear. She'd once told him that she'd nicknamed her furrow Frank. She liked to name various things. Her little secret. His, too.

The furrow soothed away. "One night."

Were they back to that? Wearily, Oliver raked a hand through his already tousled hair. "Yes, one night changed everything. I got it."

"No." Her hand fluttered in the air. The diamond ring sparkled. "Look, you changed into a wolf. I get it—life altering. But, what if you *only* change during a full moon? It was a full moon the night you were attacked, and maybe that's why you instantly shifted." Gia started to pace. "We both know nothing about werewolves."

"Most people know nothing," he growled because *werewolves aren't supposed to be real.*

"I swear, though, I feel like I watched a movie once and the shift only occurred during a full moon." She spun back to him. "If you only shift when the moon is full—that one night of the month—don't you see that we have this?"

They did *not* have this.

Her breath heaved out. "We'll get you locked up on that night. Find some secure place for you. Then you don't have to worry about hurting me—which, by the way, I don't think you would do either as man *or* wolf, but until we can prove that point, we'll play it safe." Her smile stretched. The dimple winked. "The rest of the month, you'll be completely normal! You can go about your life just like before! You can run the outdoor adventure business that you opened. I can keep operating my event planning business. We can move in together. We can get married—"

She still wanted to marry him? How the hell had he gotten so lucky and found her?

"We can do it all!" Gia proclaimed.

A faint tendril of what *could* have been hope stirred inside of him. "I haven't changed since that night." He'd only shifted one time.

A quick nod. "So maybe you won't change again until the next full moon." She did a little hop as her excitement seemed to build. "Or maybe you won't change at all, not ever again. Maybe it was a one and done event."

If only.

Gia dashed back to him. She stopped when their bodies were less than an inch apart. "I know why you came here tonight."

He'd been avoiding her since the attack. Not answering her calls. Not going to the door when she knocked at his home. A total douche move, yes, but...

I wanted her safe. It was what he always wanted. The world was dark and twisted and dangerous. Gia was a breath of sunshine. He wanted her safe above all else, and if he was the most dangerous thing she faced...*Then I can't be near her*.

"You came to break up with me."

Yes, he had. To break up with her and to leave town. He would start a new outdoor business somewhere else. Somewhere very remote, provided, of course, that he didn't wolf out and eat his customers.

Jeez, I hope that shit doesn't happen. It would be terrible for business.

"You're shutting me out because you're scared. But don't you see, Oliver? That's why you *shouldn't* shut me out. We're supposed to be partners. Us against the world, you know? So let me help you. Let's figure this thing out together." Her voice held such passionate intensity. "You aren't the only one this has happened to in the history of time—you *can't* be. We'll find the wolf that bit you."

She meant the *werewolf* that had bitten him. Because Oliver knew that had been no ordinary wolf.

"We'll find experts who know what's happening. We didn't know the supernatural score before your attack. Fine. I think we should give ourselves a pass on that one. But now that we are aware, we can find people who *do* know more. They can help us."

It wasn't *us* that needed help. It was him. She was perfect.

"One night a month—what if that's all it is? Or what if you never change again? You don't need to leave. Stay with me." She rose to her toes. Curled her hands behind his neck. Tugged him toward her. *"Stay."* Her lips brushed against his. Her mouth opened.

Her vanilla scent wrapped around him, and her taste? The sweetness was enough to make him go mad. The kiss started slowly, tenderly, but as was always the case when he kissed her, desire surged in Oliver. His hands curled around her, and he pulled her tightly against him. Her full breasts pressed to his chest, and a low moan built in her throat.

Taste.
Take.
His heart pounded faster as he kissed her deeper. Harder. He wanted to strip off her clothes and drive into Gia. He'd come to her house thinking that this was his last time to ever see her, but she was offering herself to him. Offering him hope.

He was going to take it—take *her*.

His mouth tore from hers. His hands slid under her white sweater and touched smooth, soft skin. His fingers trailed up her back, raising her sweater, and then tossing it aside. She smiled at him, sexiness personified. A white, lacy bra covered what he knew were truly sensational breasts, and he wanted her bra *gone*. A swipe of his hands, and the bra seemed to just fall away.

Wish granted.

He scooped her up—he'd always been able to hold her easily, but he didn't seem to feel her weight at all—and Oliver lifted her high so that he could clamp his mouth greedily over one breast.

She arched against him, and her short nails dug into his arms. He growled in reaction. She was so sensitive, so quick to meet his passion—so fast to drive him *wild*.

He took a few, fast steps forward and pinned her to the wall even as he turned his attention to her other breast. He greedily licked and sucked her nipple. Her moans and frantic gasps were music to his ears.

"Bedroom," she managed, her voice a husky temptation. "Let's go to—"

He wanted her naked right there. He wanted to slam into her right *there*. Because she'd been correct. He *had* come to her house that night to break things off. It had seemed the only safe choice. But if Gia was right with her ideas, if he wasn't going to turn again, or, maybe only turn on a full moon...

We can make this work. I can have her. I don't have to give up the only woman I've ever loved. And he did love her. So much that sometimes, the intensity of that love scared him.

What would I do if something happened to her? Protecting Gia was something of an obsession for him.

He carried her to the bedroom. She wrapped her legs around him. Rubbed her sex against the thick ridge of his cock. He could not wait to be driving deep and hard into her. They'd find oblivion together—maybe find it a few times. When it came to Gia, he was always insatiable.

Her bedroom was lit with soft, white Christmas lights. Gia had strung them around the four posts of her bed. That soft light was the only illumination in the room, and it just made her look even more gorgeous to him.

He put her on the bed. Grabbed her jeans. She'd already kicked off her heels, and she helped him to push those jeans over her hips and down her amazing legs. Then he reached for her panties.

They tore beneath his grip.

Somewhere, a faint whisper seemed to tease his mind.

Almost...a whisper of warning?

He ignored the warning. Oliver stripped and jumped onto the bed with her. She laughed as she reached for him. Her laugh warmed his heart. No one but Gia ever joked with him. No one but Gia could make him smile. Could make him feel like he *fit* in someplace.

Her hands slid down his chest, then trailed over his abs.

"Your body is insane," she whispered. "In case I haven't told you a thousand times, you are super hot."

He smiled. *God, Gia, I love you.*

Her fingers curled around his dick. Squeezed. Pumped. Made his eyes want to roll back into his head.

"You are super hot," she said again, "and you taste super good." She pushed him back. Crawled over him. Down him. Took the head of his cock into her mouth. Her hot, wet, driving-him-past-sanity mouth.

His hands flew out and clamped around the sheets. It was either fist the sheets or grab her—and he didn't want to grab her too hard. She was so much smaller than he was.

He heard a ripping. Ignored it.

Another strange whisper of warning seemed to trickle through his mind.

Be...careful...

She took him in deeper. His hips surged up toward her mouth. He wasn't going to last this way.

He wasn't—

Something snapped in him. A savage snarl broke from his lips, and Gia let him go. Her head jerked up. "Oliver?"

He tumbled her back onto the bed. Caught her legs. Spread them wide.

Her smile came again as she reached for him. He could see her sex. Moist and ready. He put his cock toward her and his fingers—

Claws.

His heartbeat thundered in his ears.

"Do not make me wait! You are an evil tease." She pushed her hips up toward him. "I want you!"

He wanted her. Wanted *nothing more*. But he was staring at fucking claws. His gaze flew around the bed and Oliver realized...

I cut through the sheets. When he'd been grabbing them moments before, his claws had sliced through them.

Oh, no. More sickening realization. *I cut through her panties.* He'd sliced them with his claws, not torn them.

I could fucking slice her.

"No!" Oliver jumped from the bed and spun to put his back to her. His voice had come out all wrong. Too deep. Distorted. A shudder worked over his body. He swore that he could *feel* the wolf trying to surge forward.

"Oliver?" Uncertain. "What's wrong?"

Everything. He grabbed his jeans. Managed to jerk them on, only to realize that the button had been ripped away. He'd done that. *Have to get out of here.* Oliver hurried down the hallway and ignored Gia when she called out for him.

He found her bra in the den. When he'd taken it off earlier, it had just seemed to fall away.

His fingers—*tipped with claws*—picked up the bra. The straps had been sliced straight through. *I could have sliced her just as easily. I could have cut Gia.* He hadn't even realized his claws had come out when he'd been kissing her.

Her scent hit him—so sweet and warm, and tinted with her arousal—right before he heard the fast rush of her footsteps coming behind him.

"Oliver! Tell me what's happening!"

His dick was still rock hard. He wanted her more than he wanted breath. And he had *claws*. If he took her, he'd hurt her.

Must not hurt Gia.

But her hand curled over his shoulder, and she pulled him to face her. "Look at me!"

He did.

Oliver caught the flash of shock on her face. A flash that she quickly tried to disguise, but it was too late. Swearing, he shot toward the mantel—or rather, toward the heavy, antique mirror that hung over her mantel. Oliver stared at his own reflection.

A monster stared back.

His golden eyes seemed to glow.

His cheeks were hollower, sharper.

As were his teeth.

What. The. Hell?

He slapped a hand over his mouth. A claw-tipped hand.

In the mirror, he saw Gia inching toward him. His shoulders stiffened, and he dropped his hand. "Stop."

She did. Her gaze met his in the mirror. "It's—"

"Do not tell me things are fucking okay. I was changing during sex! I cut the sheets. I cut your bra. I could have cut *you!*"

She lifted her hand, as if she'd touch him.

He whirled toward her—a move that *felt* too fast—and caught her hand in an instant. "Don't."

Tears swam in her dark eyes.

"You shouldn't want to touch me. You shouldn't want to be near me."

"I *love* you."

He loved her. That was why... "You won't see me again."

Her head shook. "No."

"I'm leaving tonight." All of this was what he'd planned to tell her before. *Before* he'd been weak and hopeful. "Going someplace remote where I can figure out what the hell is happening." Though he knew—*I'm a werewolf.* And, apparently, a werewolf who started to transform when he got horny. Fucking hell. "I will get control of the beast. I won't hurt anyone."

Hope lit her stare. "Then you'll come back?"

No, he wouldn't because...

Your control will always be weak with her. That warning whisper was in his head again, only this time, it was stronger, and Oliver knew that he was staring at his greatest weakness. "I won't be back." He looked at her hand—his fingers were still wrapped around her wrist—and the diamond ring on her delicate finger glinted. "Tell your friends and family that I'm a bastard. That I broke up with you on Christmas Eve." Because that was exactly what that night was—Christmas Eve.

"Don't do this." A desperate plea.

His gaze slid tenderly over her. His beautiful Gia. Curved and gorgeous. Funny and smart. And with a heart so tender and big that she'd opened it up to him. "You can't love the big, bad wolf."

Anger flashed on her face. "Don't tell me what I can do."

Fine. "The big, bad wolf can't love you."

A tear slid down her cheek.

He let her go. His body still ached for her, but it was nothing compared to the way his soul and heart felt. But he strode purposefully toward the door. Refused to look back even when...

"Merry Christmas, Oliver."

He opened the door. Headed out into the snow. Oliver didn't make it even five feet before the brutal shift swept over him. As he hit the snow-covered ground, he howled for what he'd lost.

CHAPTER THREE

One year later...
Mistletoe Falls, Wyoming

"Aw, someone is sad dogging it tonight, huh?"

Oliver tightened his hold on the glass before him. The last thing he needed on this nightmare of a night was for the bartender to start giving him shit. "Do not mess with me right now."

"Is it because you're a werewolf?" A wise nod, as if the fellow understood. "You guys get so touchy about the dog bit, but I mean, if it looks like a dog and it barks like a—"

Oliver's low growl stopped his words. Oliver glared at the bartender, but the fool just smiled back at him. Oliver had stumbled into this bar moments before, leaving a trail of snow in his wake. The night was a monster, the winter storm seeming to come from nowhere, and seeking shelter in the rundown bar had seemed like a good idea. Light had blazed from the faded windows and promised Oliver a bit of warmth.

Instead of warmth, he was having to deal with this jerk's BS. "I am not in the mood."

The bartender hummed and stepped closer. He also added a bit more amber liquid to Oliver's glass. "Rough night, eh?"

More like rough fucking *year*. The whole year had been shit because Oliver had lost everything that mattered to him. His *human* life. The woman he loved. He'd wound up bitten and transformed, and since then, everything good that he'd had—it had all vanished.

"Why don't you tell me about it?" The bartender was all friendly as he propped one elbow on the bar and put his chin in his hand. "Not like there are other customers waiting."

No, there weren't any others. The sole occupants of the place were Oliver and the annoying bartender. "I'm not the sharing sort."

"That's okay. I am." His smile came again. "Name's Cael."

Oliver drained his glass. He put it back down with a heavy clink and rose to his feet. His hand shoved into his pocket as he dug out some cash.

"It's on the house, Oliver."

Oliver narrowed his eyes as tension snaked through him. "How the hell do you know my name?"

A shrug. "Same way that I know you're a werewolf."

Yeah, about that...He put his hands on the bar and leaned forward. "Just how *did* you know?" Some humans were in the know, but he hadn't exactly been flashing fang and claw when he strolled inside this joint. What had tipped off the bartender?

The guy smiled. "What if I told you...I was here for you?"

Dammit. Oliver had let down his guard. He'd thought that he'd defeated the enemies on his trail, but they just kept coming. No matter what he did, they popped up over and over. Oliver drew in a bracing breath. "Then I'd say I'm sorry, but you're about to get your ass kicked."

Cael threw back his blond hair and laughed as if Oliver had just told him the most amazing joke ever.

Poor sonofabitch. He must be crazy because Oliver had *not* been kidding. He never kidded. Not since...

No, stop. You're not supposed to think about her. Even though Gia had been able to make him laugh. Only Gia.

The bartender's laughter slowly faded while Oliver waited and tapped his foot.

"Oh, no, no, no," Cael quickly said. "It's not like that at all." He poured himself a healthy drink and drained it in one chug. Then he proceeded to cough up a lung.

Oliver kept waiting, but his claws started to extend.

Cael's eyes watered. "That goes down *strong*."

"That's because you're not supposed to swallow that much at one time. Not exactly a shot glass there, genius."

Cael looked at the glass. Then back at Oliver. "I will remember that." He beamed at Oliver. "It's your lucky night."

"I don't have lucky nights." He had dangerous nights. Blood-filled nights. Death-soaked nights. Not lucky ones.

"You do tonight." Cael nodded and looked so excited that Oliver expected the guy—a fairly short fellow, and one on the thin side, one who was wearing a really shitty, out of date suit, of all things—to start bouncing. "You see, I'm your guardian angel."

Oliver waited, but there was no punchline. Figured that he *would* stumble into the one bar staffed with a madman. "This has been fun." It had not. He tossed some cash on the bar. "Good night." Oliver turned and headed for the door.

"You don't believe in angels?"

"Why the hell would I?" Oliver didn't stop.

"Well, you're a werewolf. Most humans wouldn't believe in *you*. But, seeing as how you are magical, I would have thought that you would open your mind to all of the possibilities out—*ah!*" Cael's words ended in a high-pitched scream because Oliver had bounded back across the room.

In a flash, Oliver had his razor-sharp claws at Cael's skinny throat. One swipe, and the bartender—*correction, angel*—would be missing a head. "I'm not magical." A rough, lethal snarl. "I'm a monster." *Ask anyone.*

Or...ask the person who mattered most. *Ask...her*.

His ex-fiancée.

Fuck. Why did he keep thinking about Gia? Oh, yeah, because...*one year ago, I lost her*. He damn well hated Christmas Eve.

"Even...m-monsters get guardian a-angels..."

He brought his face even closer to Cael's. "I can't decide if I should kill you or dump you in a psych ward."

Cael's mouth tightened. "How about option three?"

"I don't remember giving a third option."

"I-I'll give it." A sniff as Cael's nostrils flared. "Option three, you let me grant a wish for you."

He pulled his claws away from the *angel's* neck. "I thought genies did that bit."

"Oh, fine. You believe in them, but not in me?" Cael definitely sounded insulted. "Can't believe you're my final test. Talk about a serious challenge." He pointed at Oliver. "But I will not fail. I want them too desperately."

Okay, so the option of dumping the guy in the nearest psych ward? Looking better and better by the moment. Yet, oddly curious, Oliver heard himself ask, "What is it you want so badly?"

"My wings."

Sure. Yes. Made sense. Oliver nodded, then proceeded to jump over the bar. He grabbed the most expensive whiskey he saw from the shelves that were overflowing with liquor, yanked off the cap, and downed a satisfying gulp. "Why not?" Oliver stared into the bottle. "Not like angels are supposed to come equipped with those things."

Cael snatched the bottle away from him. "Like you're suddenly the expert on supernatural creatures? A year ago, you didn't know jack."

Tension knifed through Oliver. "I've made a point of learning plenty." During all of those sometimes brutal lessons, he'd never heard any talk of angels. "How did you know that I didn't realize paranormals existed a year ago?"

"Because!" Cael huffed as he set down the bottle and then fisted his hands on his hips. "Because I am your—"

"Guardian angel." Oliver rolled his eyes. "The angel without wings. So, does that make you like...what? An angel intern or something?"

"You have to *earn* wings, werewolf. You earn them by helping a charge. By stopping the charge from—" But he stopped. Clamped his little lips together.

Oliver could only sigh. "I am not drunk enough for the things happening this night."

"You shouldn't waste time getting drunk at all."

"Uh, huh. And what should I be doing?"

"You should be finding Gia. Staying close to her. Fighting for the life you—*ah! Would you keep those claws to yourself?*"

Oliver had his claws raised again. Oliver looked at them, then at Cael. "How do you know about—"

"Guardian. Angel." Cael pointed to himself. "Why is this concept such a challenge for you?"

Why? "Because for the last year, I've had to fight with every bit of strength I have to maintain my sanity and to keep my ass alive. Other werewolves wanted to challenge me everywhere I went. The packs all see me as an outsider because guess what? Most shifters are *born* as werewolves. They grow up in the pack. They grow up learning how to control their beasts. I'm some kind of freakish genetic throwback. My wolf only awakened when I got bitten. Because of that, the others think I'm unstable. They think I'm the enemy. They think they have to take me out."

But Cael shook his head. "They think you're something special. They're right."

Delusional. "I should have never come in this bar."

"They challenge you because you're an alpha. If they beat you, they become alpha. Only no one has beaten you...yet."

"No one will." Not being arrogant. Just stating a fact. Oliver had heard the alpha crap before. He didn't give a shit about it.

"You need a pack of your own. A family. Have you tried to—" Oliver's growl cut Cael off. "Right. Ahem. That would be why I am here." He looked up at the ceiling. "More of a warning about him would have been appreciated."

Oliver looked up. Who the fuck was Cael talking to? He just saw some cracked and peeling paint.

"What about that wish?"

His focus jerked back to Cael.

"Why not just make a wish?" Cael wheedled. "What can it hurt? If I'm crazy, nothing will happen. But if I'm the real deal, then your life will change, and you'll be super grateful to me and suddenly, I'll have wings." He pointed over his left shoulder. "They'll sprout back there. Don't you see? It's win, win."

"Nothing about this night feels like a win." He vaulted back over the bar. Shoved a stool out of his way. Once more, Oliver headed for the door. But...

What if?

"What do you have to lose?" Cael called behind him. "Just tell me...what is your fondest wish? What do you want the very most?"

His fingers hovered over the doorknob. This was total BS, but Oliver tossed an angry glare over his shoulder at Cael. The angel wanted to know what he wished for? All right. "I wish that I'd never become a werewolf."

Cael's lashes fluttered. "Oh, dear."

Seriously?

"That is *not* what I was expecting. Very, very troubling. Um..." Cael's right hand fanned his face. "How about you re-wish? A do-over? I'm sure we can make an exception in this case."

"Knew this was shit." Oliver yanked open the door. The bell over the door—a bell that he had *not* noticed before—gave a little, happy jingle. The sound seemed to jar through him. A half-forgotten memory from childhood slipped through his mind. "Did you just get wings?"

"That's not exactly how it works." Cael's sad voice. "You have to change the outcome first. Right now, I'm just granting the wish. I hope it's what you want."

Snow drifted through the doorway. Teased Oliver's face. Cooled his overheated skin. "Being human again is the only thing I want." But that wasn't really true.

She's what I want. Gia.

"Then...wish granted."

Nothing happened. There was no flash of light. No sprinkling of fairy dust or angel dust or any crap like that. There was absolutely nothing.

"As expected," Oliver muttered and marched forward.

"Come back if you need me!" Cael cried.

As if that would ever happen. Oliver stomped away as the snowfall thickened. The night had gone from bad to worse. All he wanted to do was get back to his crappy home and wait out Christmas. When the holiday passed, maybe he wouldn't feel so damn melancholy. Maybe he'd stop longing for all that he'd lost.

Except...

There was a Christmas tree lot right across the street. Oliver blinked. He didn't remember seeing the lot earlier. In fact, Oliver could have sworn that it *hadn't* been there.

He found himself hurrying toward the lights of that lot as the memory of another time—another tree lot—swirled through his mind.

The first time I met Gia. He'd rushed inside the lot because he'd needed something to perk up his house. Something to make it *feel* like a holiday.

He actually already had a damn tree at his house. One he'd put up because of *her*. A foolish impulse.

And why the hell was he suddenly rushing inside this lot? Why was he—

A big, seven-foot fir came toward him, a fir being half-carried, half-dragged by a woman with long, dark hair. Before he could move out of the way...

The tree *and* the woman barreled right into him. They all tumbled into the snow.

Chapter Four

"Oh, I am so sorry!" Gia Donato shoved away the tree and swiped at the snow and tree needles that covered the man she'd just basically knocked onto the ground. "I didn't even see you!"

He blinked at her. Her breath caught as shock rolled through her.

"Fuck me," he muttered. "Not tonight."

Gladly. Was her instant response to his invitation for a good, um, fuck. And...*any night.* But that was probably not the right thing to say so she pasted a smile on her face even as she hopped to her booted feet and offered a hand to him. "Hope you're not hurt. You, ah, caught me off-guard."

He stared at her. Way too long and awkwardly. Especially when he made *no* move to curl his hand around hers.

Okay. She pushed her offered hand against her leg. Wiped it. Was something on her? Maybe some sap?

"You don't need to look at me like I'm a freak," he growled as he jumped to his feet. Snow and more needles rained off him. "Even though we both know that's what I am."

What he was—big. Muscled. Drop-dead gorgeous. The kind of insane gorgeousness that should be reserved just for people in movies who were super airbrushed. She had never before seen anyone so gorgeous in real life. "I can't apologize for the staring," Gia told him honestly. "I was super surprised to see—"

"To see me after a year?" A wince. "I know. Look, I'm sorry. Not like I planned it. Not like I even realized you were in Mistletoe Falls. Or in this tree lot. One hell of a coincidence."

What was he talking about? "Did you hit your head?"

He raked a hand through his hair and sent snowflakes flying. "What? No?"

"Are you sure?" She moved closer to him. Stood on her tiptoes. Tried to reach for that gorgeous head of his because he was talking all crazy, and Gia was worried she'd given her handsome stranger a serious concussion. *Just my luck. Please, do not sue me.* But before she could stroke that thick, brown mane of hair, his hand caught her wrist in a lightning-fast move. "Someone has great reflexes," she murmured as her heart gave a little flutter at his touch.

His brow furrowed. "Gia, you *know* that you shouldn't touch me."

"Two things." She smiled at him and tried to ignore the fact that the little flutter had just turned into a serious nervous twist. "Thing one, why shouldn't I touch you?"

His furrow got worse.

"Thing two," Gia determinedly continued. "How do you know my name?"

He gave a rough rumble. It sounded awfully like a growl. A sexy growl. "That's not funny."

"Well, good." Her smile had to be as uncertain as she felt. "It wasn't supposed to be." Her gaze darted over him. Over what had to be at least six-foot-three inches of awesomeness. "If we'd met before, I would remember you."

"You *do* remember me. I saw the shock in your eyes when you realized who you and your tree had hit. You were shocked and horrified that you'd slammed into me."

Gia nodded. "True, I was horrified. When you act like a total klutz in front of a super-hot guy..."

He flinched. Almost looked...*pained*. Like her words had hurt him in some way. Since when was a compliment supposed to hurt? Gamely, she continued, "Um, being a klutz can be horrifying." It was also the story of her life. She'd always been tripping over her feet as a child, and no amount of dance lessons had helped, despite her mother's insistence. Gia had just knocked down lots of would-be ballerinas over the years. "I was shocked because honestly, you've got the most incredible eyes I've ever seen. I get that there are other people with golden eyes, but yours are really something quite special."

Those special eyes narrowed.

She inched back. "But you're making me uber nervous because you know my name, and you shouldn't. We *haven't* met."

He didn't speak.

Okay. She inched back a wee bit more. "So...it's late and it's cold." *And Ted Bundy was supposed to be really attractive to his victims, so how about I don't trust the good-looking guy who knows too much about me already?* Creepily too much. "I need to get this tree back home."

"But you don't live here. You live in Jasper. This isn't home."

Again, creepy. "I don't know how you realize that I previously lived in Jasper, but I do, in fact, live here now." The tale of her big move was one that she was not going to share. When it came to guys, her luck had not been stellar.

But this is a new town, a new start. I will be safe here. Once she got away from the creepy, but hot guy.

Soft snowflakes fell into her hair. She felt one touch her cheek, so Gia brushed it away. "Yes, well, it was very, um, interesting to meet you, ah—"

"Oliver."

Oh, she liked that name. Old-fashioned. Her smile came again.

"I missed your smile." Growled. "Thought about it too much."

Her gaze flew to the right. A security guard was over there, and she might just need to tell him that Oliver had a few issues going on with her—

"Here. Let me get the tree. Don't know why you're pretending we haven't met before, but the least I can do is carry the damn thing for you." Oliver wrapped one big hand around the tree and lifted it up. Surprise flashed on his face. "It's...heavy."

"Yes, that's why I was dragging it. Even someone with your..." *Glorious!* "Your, ahem, muscles will have a little trouble with it. Especially when you're just using one hand." *Maybe try two, sport.*

"But I can lift just about anything." He was staring at his hand and the tree in surprise. "My strength has been enhanced since the change."

Okay. Definitely time to leave. She wiggled her fingers toward the security officer. *A little help here.*

"The change," Oliver repeated, seemingly stunned. "Holy shit, could it be?"

The security officer waved to her. "Merry Christmas!" he called cheerily.

She wiggled her fingers at him. Harder. This was not about spreading holiday cheer. This was about wanting *assistance!*

"I don't have claws," Oliver noted.

Gia tip-toed back.

"I can control the shift now, been able to do that for months. I can make the claws appear whenever I want them to come out." He looked up at her, and a giant grin spread across his face. "Don't you see? I'm not changing anymore! Even though I am *trying* to shift."

Because what you're saying totally sounds sane. Not.

"It worked!" A cry of celebration as Oliver dropped her tree.

The security guard had finally taken the hint. He was coming closer. Good. Now if he could just haul ass a little more…

Oliver grabbed Gia's shoulders. "I'm not a werewolf anymore!"

"Fabulous. Let me go."

His hold tightened. "We can be together again!"

Nope.

"The angel granted my wish!"

Uh, oh.

The security guard was running because he'd heard Oliver's shouts. But Gia didn't wait for the guard to rescue her. She was afraid she didn't have any more time to waste. She slammed her boot into Oliver's shin as hard as she could. He gasped and staggered back. Then she whipped out her pepper spray when he lunged at her.

The spray shot straight into his eyes.

***

The bell jingled when the bar's door opened. Oliver narrowed his incredibly dry and still aching eyes as he took in the slightly fuzzy sight of Cael rubbing down the bar top—and humming happily.

Oliver slammed the door.

Cael looked up. "Oh, you're back!"

He blinked his eyes—about four times—and surged forward with determined steps.

"How'd that wish work out for you? Everything great?" Cael tapped his own shoulder. "Is someone about to get wings?"

Oliver slammed his hands down on the bar. "She doesn't *know* me."

"Who doesn't?"

"Gia."

"Who is Gia?" Cael blinked. All innocence.

An act that Oliver did not buy for even a moment. "You knew my name. You knew I was a werewolf. You are my freaking guardian angel—"

"Oh, so now you *admit* it—"

"But you expect me to believe you don't know the name of the only woman I have ever loved?" His voice rose to near shouting level.

His bad. But he was feeling stressed on account of the fact that Gia had pepper sprayed him right before she'd run *screaming* from him. She hadn't even run screaming when she'd found out that he was a werewolf the first time! But when he *wasn't* a werewolf, she and the security guard had both flipped out on him.

He would have wound up in a cell someplace if Oliver hadn't raced from the scene so quickly.

"Ah. *That* Gia." Cael nodded all sage-like.

Oliver grabbed for him.

The angel jumped back. "Settle down! It's part of the whole self-actualization and realization process! I was just getting you to verbalize for me. You know that Gia Donato is the only woman you love—the only one you have ever loved and the only one you will ever love and the only one who—"

"Who thinks I am stark, raving mad? Yes, thanks for that, by the way. Top-notch job."

Cael drew himself up to his full—what? Five-foot-three inches?—and sniffed. "I didn't make the wish. You did. Sorry if you don't like the consequences."

This was un-freaking-believable. "The consequences were supposed to be that I stopped spouting fur and howling at the moon! That I was a man, not a monster. That I wasn't a werewolf!" Yes, his voice had risen to roar-level, but no one else was in that bar, so what did it matter? "The woman I love wasn't supposed to forget me!"

Cael's head tilted. "But didn't you forget her?"

"What? No, *never.*" As if he could.

"Oh." Cael appeared confused. "But you left her. Shot out of town. Never went back. Never gave her a backward glance. I figured you'd moved on and forgotten her."

"Listen carefully. There *is* no forgetting Gia Donato. She is in my very bones. I left to protect her."

Cael tapped his chin. "Is that what you did?"

"Yes." A hiss.

"She asked you to leave to protect her?"

"No." He frowned.

"She hated that you were a werewolf?" Cael pressed. "It terrified her? Horrified her? Freaked her out?"

"No! Look, even after I was bitten, Gia still said she loved me, all right? That we could make everything work. She *loved* me, and it didn't matter and—" He stopped. Swallowed. *And I still left.* Fuck. Was this some message that Cael was trying to teach him? More freaking verbalization? For self-realization? The angel was trickier than he'd thought. And the guy was looking all smug.

Oliver narrowed his eyes. "I left to protect her," he said again.

"Uh, huh. Whatever you need to tell yourself."

"I was dangerous! I was shifting when we were about to have sex! I could have hurt her!"

"You've learned lots about werewolves in the last year. Surely, you've come across the fact that werewolves cannot hurt their own mates."

He had discovered that, yes, but...

"So why not go back to her when you learned that fun fact? Or don't you believe she's your true mate?"

He believed she was his everything. "I'm still a monster. She's still a human."

"You are stuck on that M word." Cael clicked his tongue. "But, moving on, because the problem has been solved. You aren't a monster any longer. Thanks to me."

"She doesn't know me."

Cael glanced upward. Stared hard at the peeling ceiling. "Do you see what I am working with here?" he mumbled.

Oliver clenched his back teeth.

Cael finally flicked his gaze back to Oliver. "Of course, Gia doesn't know you. Why would she?"

"Uh, because we met *before* I was a werewolf. Because I thought she'd remember that!"

Cael winced. "Oooohh. Yes, I can see where you might need a little bit more of an explanation. I will take the hit on this one. My apologies."

Oliver waited.

"I suppose," Cael mused, "I should start by telling you the occupation you have in *this* reality."

This reality? "What is it?" he gritted out.

"You're a tax attorney. You specialize in IRS tax audits."

"*What?*"

"You love math. Love it. Mad, bad love. Love audits, too. They really get your blood going."

"My blood is going plenty now, trust me." He pinched the bridge of his nose. "That's not me," he muttered. "Wearing some suit, crunching numbers all day, arguing with people from the IRS..." To him, that was hell. "I was a SEAL. Worked damn hard with my team until a bloody attack benched me." But he'd recovered from those wounds, with the aid of one hell of a lot of physical therapy. "I love being outdoors. That's why I wanted to start my outdoor adventure business after my rehab time."

"The rehab time never happened. Your time as a SEAL *never* happened. Thus, the injuries...*never* happened. And you don't like the outdoors in this reality. You prefer to stay inside. To work at your computer. To drink fine wine on the weekend and to have the best coffee in the world waiting on you in the mornings."

Oliver pinched the bridge of his nose harder.

"And you usually wear suits. You *love* your fancy suits."

He did not. "That's not me."

"Sure, it is. It's you—"

"In this reality, yes, I get that. But *why* did I change so much? I just asked not to be a werewolf! Everything else should have stayed the same."

"But that's not how life works." Cael's round jaw hardened. "Did you ever wonder why you were drawn to battle? Why you loved the rush of being a SEAL so much? Why you were willing to risk yourself over and over?"

No, he hadn't wondered. It had just been who he was.

"Ever wonder why the old you loved the outdoors? Enjoyed racing through the woods as often as possible?"

"I'm getting a bad feeling about why," Oliver rasped.

"It was because the wolf was *in* you back then. Latent, yes, but still there. The problem that you had is that you always thought the wolf was some separate being from you. He wasn't. You were still the same, your body was just different. Everything that you did in that old life, all the things you wanted, all the experiences you loved—they came from you when you carried your wolf deep inside. But to grant your wish, I had to remove him completely. So that changed everything. Ripple effect. I toss a stone and—"

"I know what a damn ripple effect is!"

A sigh. "Then why are we having this conversation?"

"*Why* doesn't Gia know me?"

"Because you weren't an outdoor adventure guy. You didn't own that business. Therefore, you never lived in Jasper, Colorado. Since you were not in Jasper, you were never at that Christmas tree lot one snowy night in order to collide with Gia Donato."

Oliver's heart hammered in his chest. "I never met her."

"You never met her." A pause. "Which is very unfortunate for her. The last year has been exceedingly difficult for Gia. She could have used someone strong at her side."

His heart hammered ever harder. "What in the hell does that mean?"

"You'll find out. When you go talk to her again. You *are* going to talk with her again, yes?"

"Hell, yes, I am." This time, he wouldn't come across as crazy. Hopefully. "Now that I know what's going on, I can play things differently."

Cael turned away to seemingly stare at the line of tequila bottles behind the bar. "Ah, yes. Try playing differently. Let's see how that works for you."

A shiver darted down his spine. "It's going to work perfectly. I got her to fall in love with me before." Determination had him lifting his chin and squaring his shoulders. "I can do it again."

Cael threw a glance over his shoulder. "Good luck with that."

Dammit. Oliver spun away and hurried for the door. When he shoved it open—

The bell jingled. He automatically shot a hard stare back at Cael.

"Not yet." Cael smiled at him. "But don't worry. I have faith in you."

Shit. Just what he needed. Oliver stormed out.

CHAPTER FIVE

"I am not crazy. I was doing a comedy scene for a local sketch group."

Gia stiffened at the deep, rumbling words. Words that were coming from *very* close by. She'd been striding down the sidewalk and admiring the festive lights that hung from the streetlamps. Those lights had distracted her, and she had not noticed *him*.

"I didn't mean to frighten you," that same rumbling voice told her. "In fact, frightening you is the last thing I intended."

She slowly turned toward the voice. Mr. Sexy Werewolf stared nervously back at her.

"My name is Oliver Abbott. I'm an—uh, I'm a tax attorney." He grimaced.

Why had he grimaced? "A tax attorney...who does sketch comedy?"

"It's, ahem, probably more improv than sketch."

"I'm supposed to buy this?" She wasn't. "You *ran* from the security guard."

"After you pepper sprayed me—which you were totally right to do, by the way—I went to wash out my eyes."

His golden eyes were rather bloodshot.

"I want you to do a background check on me," he surprised her by saying. "Run all my info and find out for yourself that I'm not a dangerous guy."

Chill bumps were on her body, and they had nothing to do with the cold. It was a busy sidewalk, lots of people were around, but she still edged back from Oliver. "Why would I want to run a background check on you? There is no need for our paths to ever cross again."

Pain slid across his face. "I wanted you to do the background check so you would know I could never be a threat to you."

Her apartment was right behind him. She'd taken the tree up earlier. Gone back down because the shop on the corner served some truly world-class hot chocolate, and she'd thought a cup would help her feel festive before she decorated. She'd sipped and savored that hot chocolate goodness before heading back to her place.

She wasn't normally the type to decorate on Christmas Eve. Usually, when the first of December rolled around, she started decking her halls. But this year had been different, harder, and instead of decking her halls, she'd packed up and fled her previous home on the first of December.

So now it was Christmas Eve. She was finally decorating and… "How did you find me?" Suspicion would not leave her alone.

He pointed down the street. "I just went to the best hot chocolate shop in town. I figured you'd be showing up, sooner or later."

"Now why would you figure that?"

"Because you love hot chocolate. You're a connoisseur."

Her eyes widened.

"Shit." *His* eyes squeezed closed. "What I meant to say was that…fuck it, I am terrifying you again, aren't I?"

"Creeping me out, definitely. You just admitted to stalking me to the hot chocolate shop, and listen, Oliver…I cannot deal with another stalker right now."

His eyes flew open. "Another?"

"Yes. Another. So let me just tell you what's going to happen." She released a deep breath. "You're going to walk away from me. You are not ever going to come close to me again. Because if you do, I *will* be calling the cops. One man almost ruined my life, and I am not going through that again. I just found a safe haven here and I—" She stopped. Frowned. Shifted a bit so that she could see around Oliver.

Oh, God. That figure behind him…that *familiar* figure. "He found me." He was coming out of her apartment building. Rushing toward her in his long, billowing, black coat.

"What? Who found you?" Oliver questioned quickly. "Gia, why do you look so scared? What's—"

"Gun!" she screamed. "Behind you!"

Oliver started to turn toward the shooter.

It was too late.

Her stalker yelled, "He won't take you away from me! I told you before, you belong to me, Gia. You're mine. *Mine.*"

The bullet fired.

She tried to shove Oliver out of the way. This wasn't his fight. But he was big and heavy and the bullet tore into him. She heard his grunt. Felt his surge of surprise but then...

Pain. Burning and twisting inside of her. Gia glanced down at her chest. At the blood. The bullet had gone through Oliver and into her. It hurt so much. More than anything had ever hurt before.

She fell back and hit the sidewalk. Her head slammed into the cement. She stared straight up as screams filled the air around her. Her body was ice-cold everywhere but her chest. Her chest was so hot.

Footsteps pounded.

The shooter was fleeing.

Snowflakes fell onto her cheeks.

***

Some sonofabitch had just shot him!

Oliver slapped a hand to his side. The bullet had blasted right through him. Hurt like a mother. He'd had worse, though, back in his SEAL days, so he knew the wound wasn't gonna be lethal, and he started to surge after the asshole who was already racing away. He hadn't gotten a good look at the man. Tall, wide shoulders, wearing a black coat.

"H-help…" Weak. Low.

Gia?

He spun around. She was on the ground, her dark hair spread out and her terrified eyes staring straight up. Her body trembled as she tried to lift her hand and touch her chest. Her blood-covered chest. "No!" The roar of denial burst from him.

The shooter's footsteps thudded away.

People were screaming around him. Some crowded closer. Some ran away.

"Call an ambulance," Oliver bellowed as he fell to his knees beside Gia. He didn't even feel his injury. All he could focus on in that instant—it was her.

His Gia, bleeding out right before him.

He tried to examine her wound. *Fuck. No.* It was bad. So bad. "Ambulance!" he thundered once more. But in the back of his mind, he was already afraid that it wouldn't arrive in time.

Time…God, I wasted so much time. A whole year when I could have been with her.

He put his hands on her wound. Tried to stop that terrible flow of blood. Her blood instantly soaked his fingers. "Baby, hold on!" Oliver was begging. He knew it. Didn't care. "Please, Gia, hold on! Do not leave me! Do not! *Please!*"

Her gaze fluttered toward him. Her dark, beautiful gaze. Confused. Pain-filled.

"I love you, Gia." Tears pricked at his eyes. "I love you, and I just found you again, and I can't lose you!"

But she shook her head. "You...d-don't...know...m-me..."

More blood. As if just speaking had made her wound worse. "I know you," he told her quickly. "You love hot chocolate even when it's July, and you put ornaments on your tree that you've collected from every vacation that you've ever taken. You sleep late on Saturday, but you wake up early on Sunday because you like to get every last drop out of the weekend that you possibly can and you—"

Her dark eyes were still on him. But...the light that had been in her eyes was fading. The light that was *Gia* was fading.

"You call the fucking furrow between your brows Frank! You name everything!"

Her breath hitched.

"Please, don't! Don't leave me. Baby, don't go! Don't—"

Her lashes fell.

The snow came down harder. The white flakes mixed with her blood. And on that sidewalk, with a dozen strangers around him, the woman that Oliver loved more than life itself...she died beneath his hands.

CHAPTER SIX

The bell jingled—an angry, short sound as the bar door flew open and slammed into the wall. Snow swirled inside as Oliver stormed toward his devil of a guardian angel. "She's gone."

Cael gave a little burp and not-so-discreetly shoved away the glass of whiskey that was close to him. "Who is? And where did she go?"

He stalked toward the bar. Grabbed the whiskey glass. Threw it against the nearest wall. It shattered into a million pieces. The same way he'd shattered on that blood-soaked sidewalk. "Gia is gone. She's dead."

Cael's eyes widened. "You don't say."

"Yes," he gritted out between clenched teeth. "I fucking say. She's dead, and now, so are you." He reached for the bastard.

Cael shot back. A very, very fast move. "But I didn't hurt her!"

"You're not an angel. An angel wouldn't let someone like Gia die. Someone good. Someone innocent. Someone who freaking baked brownies for the homeless on Christmas and kept extra socks in her glove compartment because she said that you never knew when you'd see someone on the street who needed socks." His hands were shaking, so he balled them into fists. "You're not an angel," he repeated. "You're some kind of demon. Or maybe you *are* the devil. You're playing with my head. Giving me my worst nightmare when you promised to grant my fondest wish."

"There you go again," Cael huffed. "Blaming me because you don't like the way the wish turned out."

"Gia died beneath my hands! I loved her, and she's gone."

"Well, if you loved her, then maybe you shouldn't have left her alone. Maybe you should have been there sooner, and you could have protected her from the threat that's been waiting."

He wasn't playing any more games. "Bring her back."

"Uh, it doesn't quite work that way."

Yes, it did. "Bring. Her. Back." He reached for the bottle of whiskey that was still on the counter.

"I'm not scared of you," Cael said, and his voice only trembled a little. "You're not a werewolf any longer. You're a human. You don't have claws—"

Oliver smashed the bottle on the side of the bar. "What I've got is jagged glass, and I'm betting it cuts as good as the claws ever did."

Alarm flashed on Cael's face. "Let's just both calm down."

"Bring. Her. *Back*."

"I *can't!* That's not how it works! You tell me your greatest wish—the thing you want most in the world—and I help you get that wish! What you wanted was to be human. Well, wish granted. You're human, and when you're human? Well, bullets can tear through your skin. They can slam right through you and then rip into the heart of the woman that you love."

Grief nearly choked Oliver.

"When you're human," Cael continued grimly, "your reflexes are normal. Not super-fast and enhanced. You can't whirl to face an attacker or grab your girlfriend and push her out of the way before the bullet comes flying to end her life."

"She didn't even know me at the end," he rasped. The pain would not stop. "She stared at me as if I was nothing more than a stranger." To her, he had been.

"When you're human..." Cael's voice was lower. Softer. Sadder. "Your senses aren't enhanced. You don't hear the attacker coming until it's too late. But if you had only been a werewolf..."

Oliver's shoulders stiffened. "A werewolf could have saved her."

A nod. "The odds of her living would have been much higher, certainly."

"*I* could have saved her."

"Not human you. But that werewolf version? The one *you* hated but that Gia was willing to accept even though she knew nothing about paranormals? Yes, I think it's quite possible, even probable, that he would have done a much better job of protecting her."

Hope burned in Oliver. Burned past the suffocating grief and the consuming pain and the choking rage. "Turn me back."

Cael inched closer to the bar. "What's that? Not sure I understood."

"You understood. Now turn me back."

Cael sighed. "Make me human. Make me a werewolf. Someone is so demanding. I granted your fondest wish—"

"That wasn't my freaking fondest wish! I thought I could only go back to her if I was human." The words flew out with the pounding force of his desperation. "Being with her—being with Gia *is* the only thing I want. I want to hold her at night and wake up with her in the morning. I want to haul fucking giant Christmas trees all the way across town for her. I want to kiss her under the mistletoe, and I want to hear her laugh." He *missed* her laugh so much. "I want Gia."

Cael leaned across the bar. Patted a hand on Oliver's shoulder. "Was that so hard?"

He growled.

"Oh, look." Bright. Perky. "Almost sounds like you're turning back already."

He hadn't changed at all. "Fix me."

Cael shrugged. "Fix it all yourself."

Why that arrogant, tricky, bast—

Before he could shout or swing or do anything else...darkness closed over Oliver.

***

A hand patted Oliver on the shoulder.

"Fix it," Oliver muttered.

"Sorry, buddy, but you need to wake the hell up."

His body jerked. Oliver realized that his head was on the bar top, his body slumped forward. He heaved upright, and his gaze slammed into the bartender's.

The little guy squinted back at him. "You okay?"

"No, Cael," he snapped. "I am *not* okay. I asked you to fix my life. To turn me back into a werewolf and—"

The bartender stared at him as if he'd grown two heads. "Ah, I think you've had enough to drink for the night."

A glass of whiskey sat beside Oliver. A perfectly normal, unshattered glass.

"Want me to call you a cab?" the bartender asked.

"I *want* to be a werewolf again!" Oliver snapped. His hand slammed into the bar. "Why won't you just—" He'd caught sight of his hands. And the claws that tipped his fingertips.

He was back. *Back, baby*. His gaze jumped back to Cael.

"You have claws," he pointed out, voice nervous.

"Cael, I could kiss you right now."

Cael firmly shook his head. "I am in a relationship. And...*how* do you know my name? We didn't exactly exchange a lot of personal info before you started snoring on my bar."

Snoring on his bar? Wait, had all of that just been a dream? No way. *No. Way.* "Nice try, angel, but I'm not buying it."

"Should I call someone for you?" Cael asked delicately.

He threw cash onto the bar. "Gia moved to this town, didn't she? And she's in danger. I'll find her, don't you worry."

"Um...good?"

"I'll find her, I'll protect her, and I'll love her forever." He exhaled. Squared his shoulders. "Then you can get your precious wings and fly to any place you want." With that, Oliver practically leapt for the door. But right before he opened it...

Oliver glanced back.

And he caught the smile on Cael's face before the angel could wipe it away.

Cael really sucked at trying to look innocent.

"Thank you," Oliver told Cael.

He opened the door. The bell jingled.

***

Cael waited until the door closed before he smiled again. The bell seemed to echo around him, and for a moment, he could have sworn that he felt a little tickle begin behind his left shoulder blade.

CHAPTER SEVEN

Someone knocked on her apartment door. A very, very insistent knock. No, more like a fierce pounding. Gia jumped at the sound, and the glass ornament she'd just been about to hang on the tree slipped from her fingers and shattered on the wooden floor.

The knocking continued.

He hasn't found me. He couldn't have found me. She tip-toed toward the door. Pressed her hand to the wood and put her eye to the little peephole.

When she saw her visitor, the wave of shock that hit her had Gia nearly falling to the floor just like the ornament. Falling and shattering. Instead, she managed to stay upright, and she yanked open the door. "What in the hell are you doing here?"

Oliver stood on the threshold. Even bigger than she remembered. Even better looking, too, as if the last year had been some magical walk in the park. His chest was heaving as he sucked in fierce breaths, and he stared at her like he'd just found the most perfect Christmas gift ever.

Oh, wait. That's probably how I'm staring at him. She twisted her features into a glare.

But then he said—

"Thank God, you're alive."

"What?"

He grabbed her. Yanked her into a fierce, nearly bone-crushing hug as he held her against him, and Oliver shuddered.

He was warm and strong, and he smelled like home, damn him. He smelled like *her* home. She wanted to snuggle against him, hold on tight and never let go, but *he* was the one who'd let go before. He was the one who'd left her and just vanished, and she hadn't been able to find him no matter how hard she searched.

"I still have time," he muttered as he kissed her forehead. Her temple. Her cheek. Any place he could reach. "I can still have you." Then he kissed her on the mouth. A passionate, wild, consuming kiss that sparked a floodgate of desire inside of her. He'd always been able to ignite her need so easily. Always been able to make lust burn with just a touch.

Plus, it had been one very long year. One very lonely year because she hadn't been able to bear the thought of anyone but him and—

She tore her mouth from his. "No!" Gia shoved against the chest she'd always loved and drooled over. "You don't get me. We're over." She staggered back a few steps and could still taste him, dammit. "I don't know how the hell you found me—"

"An angel in a bar."

Gia squinted at him. No, there had been no way he'd said what she just thought. Doggedly, she continued, "But you do *not* get to waltz back into my life like the last year didn't happen. You left *me*." He'd ripped out her heart and stomped on it. "I tried to find you." Because, apparently, she was a glutton for punishment. "But it was as if you'd never existed. Your old SEAL buddies wouldn't even talk to me, though I was sure some of them were helping you to hide. Months passed, and there was no phone call, no text, no letter." *No you.* "I moved on. You do *not* get to come back and start kissing me like nothing happened."

"Gia, I—"

She slammed the door in his face. Locked it.

And then she let the tears fall.

***

Oliver could hear the sound of her cries. Soft and muted because Gia never wanted anyone to hear or see her cry. *I did this to her.* His hands pressed to the wood. "I am going to fix this," he promised her.

He was. He would not give up. He would apologize a million times. Get down on his knees, but he wasn't going to give up. Oliver knew he could *not* give up.

Before he'd become a werewolf, there was no way he would have believed that Cael and everything that had happened that night was real. He would have blown it all off. Said it was some drunken dream.

He wasn't the same man any longer. He knew about magic, and Oliver understood that being a werewolf—it was something he needed to be. *I can protect her this way.*

But first, he had to get back into her life. Step one of that plan? Getting past her locked door.

"I'm sorry," he said again, his words clear and loud.

Then he turned and walked away.

***

Gia swiped at her cheeks. She hated crying. It just led to headaches and blotchy, red skin. She was *not* a pretty crier, never had been.

"I'm sorry." His voice seemed to reverberate through the door.

She sucked in a bracing breath before she flipped the lock once more—this time to *unlock it*—and wrenched open the door. If he had some big apology, then he could just shove it up his—

Gone.

The hallway was empty. As if Oliver had never been there at all.

Her lower lip trembled. She wrapped her right arm around her waist, crept back, and quietly shut the door.

***

Fifteen minutes later...

Someone was knocking at her apartment door.

Gia's shoulders stiffened. She'd just climbed onto the stepladder so that she could put her star on the tree. Her eyes were dry, her cheeks puffy, and her head ached.

The knocking came again. Not insistent like before, but more careful and cautious. Keeping the star in her hand, she slowly backed down the steps. Then she made her way to the door. She took time to glance through the peephole.

This time, she was more prepared. Her knees barely trembled. She opened the door.

Oliver had his hands behind his back. His expression was so tender, almost reverent, as he stared at her.

Do not weaken. "I don't want you knocking on my door all night long. I have things to do."

His gaze darted to the star. "Would you like some help?"

No, she would not. "Go away."

His shoulders rolled, and one hand moved from behind his back as he brought a bright red cup toward her. "How about some hot chocolate? Would that help? I bought it from the shop on the corner, and I know you think they've got the best stuff in town."

How did he know that? *Lucky guess.* Had to be. "Do you honestly think that one cup of hot chocolate is going to buy my forgiveness?"

His second hand slid from behind his back. "What about two?" This cup was green.

She stared at the two offerings. "How were you even knocking on the door?"

"I used my elbow."

Gia would *not* smile at him. "I'll take the hot chocolate. *One* cup." She did. Her free hand curled around it, but in the process, her fingers brushed his. A spark of awareness flooded through her. A spark? Who was she kidding? More like a wildfire of awareness flooded through her. But she pulled back with her precious hot chocolate, and the cup was wonderfully warm in her grasp.

"Please, let me come in."

Her head tilted. "If I don't, are you going to huff and puff until you blow my door down?"

"No." He stared straight at her. "But I will just stay in the hallway, and I'll drink my hot chocolate. I will stay close because there is nothing that can make me leave you."

Really? He'd been fast enough to leave her before. Head-spinningly fast.

"You're in danger. He's followed you here, Gia."

Her hand jerked. Good thing there was one of those snap-on tops covering the hot chocolate. Otherwise, she would have sent the precious liquid flying everywhere. "Wh-what are you talking about?"

"He's going to come for you tonight, sweetheart. He's going to try and kill you, but I swear, that will not happen." Oliver's jaw hardened. "He won't get through me this time."

This time?

"I will keep you safe. I will do whatever it takes, but you will not be dying tonight."

Wow. Her jaw dropped. Hurriedly, she snapped it closed before eventually managing to croak, "Did you just say I was dying tonight?"

"Only over *my* dead body."

Her heart thundered. She looked to the left, to the right. The hallway was empty. But this was still no place to have this particular talk. "Come inside."

"Thought you'd never ask."

Her eyes narrowed, but she backed up. She let him inside. Then flipped her lock again. She led the way to the den and stopped only long enough to take a few fortifying sips of her hot chocolate. *Heaven on earth.* Then she put the cup down, placing her star on the table next to it before spinning to face Oliver.

Big, gorgeous, sexy, heartbreaking Oliver. Oliver who seemed to know so many things that he shouldn't and who had to be *wrong* about her dying. Right? "Talk." Gia crossed her arms over her chest.

But he was taking his time and strolling around her small den. Poking and prodding at things. He'd put down the other cup of hot chocolate and had lifted up a photo frame. A photo of—dang it all—them. "Surprised you still wanted to see me."

"What did you think I would do? Act like you never existed?" Her response was clipped. "You made me happy. I like to keep memories of happy times."

He looked over at her. "All of my happy times were with you."

Do not weaken. "Right up until the moment you ran out of on me."

"I was shifting while we were making love. Thought I'd hurt you. Thought it would never be safe for you to be around me." He glanced back at the photo. It had been taken on one of their many hiking trips. She knew they were hugging each other and grinning from ear to ear. Longing flashed on his face as he stared at the photo. "All I wanted was for you to have a happy, *normal* life."

And all I wanted was to be with you.

With care, he put down the frame. Squared his shoulders and faced her. "You weren't scared of me, were you?" He stalked toward her.

She stood in front of the tree.

"Even with claws, even with fangs, you still wanted to be with me."

"That's kind of what love is. Being there when things are easy? Anyone can do that. But staying when things get difficult—or, furry, as in your case—that's what it means to truly love someone." Her chin lifted. "I truly loved you. I would have done anything for you."

Oliver flinched. "You're using the past tense."

She was. Deliberately. To make her point.

"Let me be clear." His voice deepened ever more and rolled through her. "I truly love you, Gia. I always have. I love you so much that I left when all I ever wanted to do was spend every single day of my life at your side. I left because I couldn't bear the thought of so much as scratching your skin." His hand rose, and the back of his knuckles trailed lightly over her cheek. "Your perfect, silken skin."

She shivered. "Did you magically stop shifting? Did you find some miraculous cure? Is that why you're back now?"

"No. I will be a werewolf forever, just as I will love you forever."

Gia choked down the lump in her throat.

"But I don't have to worry that I will hurt you any longer. I learned that a werewolf *can't* physically hurt his true mate. My claws or my fangs won't ever be used against you."

"What in the hell is a true mate?"

"It's the person you love above all others. The person who owns your heart and who owns you. The person who makes you feel good just by existing. The person you would sacrifice *anything* for."

Another swallow because that stupid lump had risen again. "You just gained this amazing knowledge that it was safe to be with me...when, tonight?" And he'd rushed to her door?

A shake of his head.

Her eyes narrowed. "When?" Bit out.

"Six months ago."

Six months and he hadn't come to find her—

"But I was being hunted by a pack out of El Paso at the time. Turns out, I'm something of an unusual beast."

"Tell me about it," she muttered. He was still touching her cheek, almost as if he couldn't help himself. She was still letting him, almost as if she couldn't help herself. *I missed his touch.*

"Werewolves are born. They shift when they hit puberty. Only a very few are latents—they have the genes, but the wolf was so far back in the family tree that they don't ever transform, unless something happens."

This was all news to her. She'd tried to learn more about werewolves, but when she'd made her inquiries—over and over again—the people she'd spoken with had all acted as if she was crazy. Though she suspected many of them had been faking the reaction. They just hadn't wanted to talk to her because she was human.

"The bite changed things for me. The night I was attacked, that wasn't an ordinary wolf. It was a werewolf. The bite sent me into an immediate shift. I'm...according to some, I'm an alpha. That means other wolves like to challenge me for dominance, and I have to kick their asses." A pause. "A lot. So while the line of challengers was chasing me down, going to you wasn't something I could do."

"You are such a liar." Her hands flew to her hips. Fisted. "If you wanted me, you could have come to me."

His hand fell. "I *always* want you. But I also wanted you safe and happy. Living a normal life seemed like it would be best."

"Do *not* tell me what's best for me!" Gia exploded. "You don't know! *I* know! And being abandoned by the man I love?" Shit, she'd slipped and used present tense. "*Loved*," Gia corrected angrily. "Being abandoned by the man I loved is not the best. It's the worst. You have no idea what

I have been through in the past year without you!" She would *not* cry again.

"I know." Grim.

Gia shook her head.

"I found out tonight. *That's* why I'm back. Because there is a threat to you that *cannot* be allowed to stand. If I had known about him sooner, I would have instantly come to your side. Your safety has always been what mattered most to me. I left to protect you. I stayed gone to protect you. Now I'm back—"

"To protect me?" she finished, trying for a flippant tone but failing miserably.

A nod.

"How dare you?" Pain and rage twisted through her. "Why couldn't you just come back because you can't live without me? Because the world goes dark if I'm not at your side? Because you love me so much that getting through each day without me at your side rips you apart?" Because that was how it had felt for her. But she'd lived through the pain. She'd moved on. Even as danger had slipped deeper into her life.

A shudder rippled his big frame. "The world does go dark without you. Every single day without you by my side ripped out *my* heart. The idea of living without you? Let's just say I know too well what this world would be like if you weren't here—not just gone from my life because you're off being happy somewhere else, but what it would be like if you were *gone* completely—"

She blinked at the rough grief that thickened his voice.

"And I *know* I can't live in a world that doesn't have you in it. I love you. I loved you before, I love you now, and I will love you until the moment that I take my last breath. You're it for me, and if you give me a chance—please, baby, please, give me a chance," desperate and rough, "then I can show you a whole new life. I can prove myself to you."

She didn't want a new life. She didn't want some dream. "Crazy werewolf," Gia said as her whole body leaned toward him. "All I want is my life back with you."

He pulled her against him.

She wrapped her arms around him.

And she kissed him.

CHAPTER EIGHT

Gia was alive. Alive and beautiful and warm and in his arms. She was kissing him and stroking his arms and shoulders. Murmuring that she'd "missed him, dammit" and to "not ever do stupid shit again" as their mouths met and released in wild kisses.

Part of him feared that this was a dream. Another vision to drive him mad. But even if it was just a vision, Oliver wasn't going to let her go. He was taking her because he'd longed for her so many days and nights. When the change would sweep over him and his bones would break and the beast would howl, she'd been the only thing that got him through that hell. He would think of her. Imagine her. And he could have peace.

"I shouldn't do this," Gia said as her head pulled back. Her lips were swollen from his desperate kisses. Her dark eyes gleaming with a need to match his own. "But I've missed you so much. What could once hurt? For old time's sake?"

"Not just once." He wanted forever. He'd get it. But if she wanted to take things one day—or one fuck—at a time, they'd do it. They would do whatever she wanted. "I love you," he told her. She needed to understand exactly how he felt.

She kissed him again.

He should take her to her bedroom, wherever that was. Carry her and be amazing. Sweep her off her feet. Caress her and give her a dozen orgasms with his hands and his mouth.

And he'd do that...

After I get control back.

Because his control was broken. Shattered. The memory of her *dying* in his arms, of the wrenching pain that had nearly destroyed him beat at his mind. Oliver had to be sure Gia was safe. Alive. He had to feel her all around him. Needed to hear her moans and see her pleasure. Needed to *feel* all of her.

So he stripped her right there. Beneath the lights of her Christmas tree. The scent of pine filled the air. Soft Christmas music drifted from her speakers—he'd noticed the light music when he first followed her into the apartment. Her clothes hit the floor, and he realized...

"Sorry," Oliver gasped because his claws had just cut through the straps of her bra.

She looked at the bra on the floor. Then back up at him. "You didn't cut me."

"I would *never*."

"Glad you finally realize that." She kicked away her shoes and jeans and underwear and— "Thought this would save me from getting my clothes slashed."

Gia was naked. Her body gleamed like the best present in the world beneath those lights. Her breasts were full, her nipples tight and hard, and he needed them in his mouth. His hands—tipped with claws—curled around her waist, and he lifted her up against him. Lifted her high and didn't feel her weight at all because his enhanced strength was back. He took a nipple into his mouth and licked her and sucked her and had her squirming against him.

Then he gave the second nipple the same sensual attention. Her nails sank into his shoulders as she moaned and demanded more.

He'd give her more. More and more always.

His cock shoved at the front of his jeans. Gia had pushed away his coat, but he still had on his shirt and jeans. They needed to go, ASAP.

He pushed her against the nearest wall. Caged her there with one hand on her hip as his other dipped between her legs. She was wet and hot. "There...hasn't been anyone else for me," he told her roughly. Oliver wanted her to understand. "There will always...only be you."

Her long lashes lifted. "No one else for me. Even when I was pissed and considered going out to find a revenge fuck."

A growl tore from him. His touch became harder, more possessive.

"Like I could do that," she whispered. "Not who I am. And I only wanted you."

He would die wanting her. But for now, he'd be fucking her.

Her hands slid between them. Jerked open the button and zipper on his jeans. His cock sprang into her hot hands, and she stroked him. Pumped him and squeezed. His teeth snapped together. "*Gia...*"

"We'll go slow on the second round. Maybe the third," she amended breathlessly. "But for now, it's been a long time, and I really need you." She did a shimmy, angled her hips, and the head of his cock pushed at the tender opening of her body. "Oliver?"

He looked into her eyes. Saw his world. She stared back at him with faith. Trust. He knew his own eyes would be glowing with the power of the beast. The wolf wanted her—because *he* was the beast. Cael had been right on that. In the form of man or wolf, Oliver was the same.

And she was his.

He sank into her. Sank as deep as he could go and they both shuddered because it had been too long and the sex between them had always been too good. There was no more talking. There was only the thud of flesh. Pounding and need. Kisses that took and lust that ignited hotter and hotter with every moment. Her breath panted out. His cock drove relentlessly into her and when she came, he felt the sudden contraction of her core as she squeezed his dick. Her mouth parted, and Gia choked out his name as the pleasure lashed across her face and tightened her body.

He kept thrusting, wanting to make the orgasm even stronger for her. Wanting to give her everything. Just as she gave him *everything*. His orgasm exploded through his body, the powerful release rippling through every nerve and cell, and Oliver roared her name.

Her neighbors probably freaking hated them, but at that moment, he couldn't care. All he could do was hold onto her as tightly as he could...

And since he was a werewolf, that was pretty damn tight.

***

Gia opened her eyes. She was in bed. Darkness was all around her. Her body ached in an ever-so-wonderful way, but for just a moment, she was afraid.

Fear wasn't new. For the past few months, she'd often woken afraid. Afraid that *he'd* do something else. Afraid that an attack would come.

But this fear was different. This time, Gia feared...*Was it a dream?*

The door squeaked open. She jerked upright even as a frightened cry rose to her lips—

"Baby?" Oliver's voice. His warm, rich, wonderful voice. The voice she'd missed over the last year. "I was just making sure all of the doors and windows were locked. I was coming right back."

No dream.

Light trickled into the room from the open door. Part of her—a very, very big part—wanted to just lift her hand to Oliver in invitation and pull him into the bed with her. She remembered now that he'd carried her into the bed after the amazing sex in the den. Carried her in there and tucked her under the covers as if she was something precious to him.

She'd drifted off to sleep moments later because she'd felt safe for the first time in a while. But...

She didn't offer her hand to him because while that was a temptation, Gia knew that they needed to talk. One of those big, life-changing talks. So she sat up. Tucked the sheet beneath her arms and made sure it covered her naked breasts. Once she was satisfied that she wouldn't go flashing Oliver, she reached over to turn on the lamp.

He wore jeans as he stood in her bedroom doorway. Jeans and nothing else. His chest was even more muscled than she remembered. Lickable, killer abs. A body made for sin. And danger.

Do not drool. "We need to talk." Yes, she'd jumped onto him in the den. A Christmas Eve sex weakness? Or a just weakness for the one man she loved? Didn't matter. There were bigger issues at play... "How do you know I'm in danger? You haven't been in my life. You *shouldn't* know."

His head dipped down.

She held her breath as she waited for his answer.

The silence and tension in the room ticked past. "Gia..." He finally raised his head and looked at her. "Do you believe in angels?"

She considered the question. "Of course." No hesitation.

He blinked in surprise.

Gia had to laugh. "My lover is a werewolf. Did you seriously think I wouldn't believe in *angels?*"

"Cael would freaking love you," Oliver said as he took several quick steps toward the bed.

She tensed. "Who is Cael?"

"My guardian angel. Or, rather, my *wannabe* guardian angel. Maybe he was an angel intern, never did get the full title for the guy. If things work out with me, he's supposed to get his wings." Oliver raked a hand over his face. "He's the reason I know you're in danger. He gave me a glimpse earlier tonight."

"A glimpse of what?" Gia was trying to follow along, but he'd lost her.

"A glimpse of what could happen if I got my wish. See, I wandered into his bar, and he was there."

"Okay. You went into a bar and met an angel." Her nostrils flared. "This had better not be a joke because it feels like a joke, and I am *not* in the mood."

He sat on the edge of the bed. The mattress dipped. "We both know I can't tell jokes for shit. The only person in the world who can ever make me really laugh and smile—it's you."

That was sweet.

His hand rose. Curled under her chin. Held her so carefully. "He asked me to make a wish. I wished that I hadn't been a werewolf."

"Guessing that wish didn't come true," she managed to say. "Because I did catch sight of the claws earlier." The claws. The sharper teeth. The glowing eyes. She'd even felt his muscles stretching and hardening all over. The wolf had been present when they made love, but she hadn't been scared.

She'd never been scared of him.

"I had a glimpse," he said again. "In that glimpse, you were there."

She waited for more.

But he was just staring into her eyes. "You're the most beautiful thing in my world. Always have been."

She smiled. "Focus, Oliver."

His gaze slid to her cheek. "I missed that dimple."

"The dimple missed you, too, but focus."

His smile slipped out. It made her heart do a funny flutter because he had always seemed to smile so easily with her. She hadn't even realized he was different with other people, not until later in their relationship.

A jerky nod from him. "Focus. I'm trying. I just missed you so damn much."

And I missed you. "You were saying I was 'there'—but where is that? I don't understand."

"You were in the glimpse. I thought if I could be just a human, I could go back to you. I wouldn't be a freak, and you'd want me again."

Her hands lifted quickly, and the sheet almost dropped. She pressed her palms to his stubble-covered cheeks. "Listen carefully. I *never* thought you were a freak, and I have always wanted you."

She felt the sheet inching down, so she let him go. Adjusted things.

Oliver exhaled. "I was shown what would happen if I lost the wolf. In the glimpse, you were here, in Mistletoe Falls."

"Well, I did recently move here so..."

"I met you at the Christmas tree lot down the road earlier tonight. You were picking out your tree."

A shiver slid over her. "I *was* at the tree lot earlier tonight. It's where I got Clark W. Griswold." *Her* tradition. Kind of weird and off-kilter, but it was what it was. She always named her Christmas trees after favorite characters from holiday movies. "I was there, but you weren't."

His jaw firmed. "I met you there." A slight pause. "I terrified you there."

She laughed.

He didn't. "You pepper sprayed me. You didn't know me. Because I wasn't a werewolf, we'd never met."

"Uh, yeah..." Now she was starting to worry. "Did you hit your head tonight? Because we met long before you became a werewolf."

"Turns out, the whole life I had was *because* I was a werewolf, whether latent or not. You take the wolf away, and everything changed. There was never an us, and I was a tax attorney. Apparently, I had quite a collection of suits, and I loved audits."

A laugh exploded from her.

"That shit is not funny," he groused. "Know what else isn't funny? You ran from me. I found you later so I could explain, or *try* to explain the craziness but..." His voice trailed away.

"Don't leave me hanging on the good part."

"We were on the sidewalk outside of your building. You'd gone to the hot chocolate shop right down the road and were coming home. I stopped you and we were talking, but then I saw fear on your face."

"I was scared of you?"

"You were scared of the man behind me," Oliver told her flatly. "The man with the gun. The man who shot and killed you while I was *right there.*"

CHAPTER NINE

She hadn't heard him correctly. Gia shook her head.

"He was a big sonofabitch. Probably close to my height. Broad shoulders. He was wearing a black coat, heavy and long, and he had dark hair. I caught a glimpse of it as he ran away, but then I heard you asking for help..."

Her chest felt tight.

"You'd seen him, and you realized he had a gun. You tried to shove me out of the way." The beast flared to life in his eyes. "But when he fired, the bullet just went through me and into you."

No, not happening. She climbed over him, nearly fell out of the bed, and managed to drag the sheet with her. Gia wrapped it around her body as her knees knocked together.

"I wanted to chase him and kill him, but you called for help. That was when I realized you'd been hit. I tried to help you." His hands fisted as he rose to stare at her. "Your blood just seeped through my fingers, and you died, staring at me like I was a stranger."

Her toes curled against the hardwood floor. "This can't be happening."

"I know it sounds crazy, but it's true. Cael is an angel, and he showed me a glimpse, and you're in danger and—"

"No." She ran to the window. Peered through the blinds. Snow was falling, and the street below appeared empty. "I mean, he can't have found me. I didn't leave a trace behind when I left Jasper. I didn't tell anyone where I was going. I just packed up my car, and I drove until I found this town." Because it had felt right. Some instinct had almost whispered...

Home.

The floor creaked as Oliver moved to stand behind her. "Who is he?"

She didn't see anyone below. "He can't have found me," she repeated.

"I couldn't see his face. As soon as he fired the weapon, he turned and ran, and he was very fast. Tell me who he is." His hand curled over her shoulder. "Tell me, and I'll end him."

She looked down at his hand and saw that his claws had come out. "This isn't your fight."

"The hell it isn't. He's coming after *you.*"

"He's been coming after me for a very long time. Since before I ever met you. But back then, I thought a simple restraining order would be enough to stop him. For a while, it was. He was out of my life, actually, the whole time that you and I were together." She turned toward him as his hand fell away. "It was only after you left that I started to realize he was still watching me. Then he did more than watch. The phone calls began. The flowers started arriving." Nothing too bad, not at first. "The doors were unlocked at my home to show me that he'd been inside." A tear slid down her cheek. "The windows of my car were smashed. Then the last night I was in Jasper—the night he caught me in the park—I felt what I'm sure was a knife pressed to my throat."

A growl built in Oliver's throat.

"If a group of teenagers hadn't walked by, I think he would have killed me." She didn't mention that it had been the same park where Oliver had proposed to her. That she'd often walk in that park because that place was her last memory of being truly happy. She also didn't mention that the diamond engagement ring was in the top drawer of her nightstand. She hadn't worn it since Oliver had vanished, but she also hadn't been able to sell it or give it away.

"A name, Gia. I want his name."

"Darren. Darren Emmanuel."

She saw the flash of recognition in his eyes and inclined her head. "Yes, the real estate mogul. He looks out at the world, and he once told me he wanted to own everything beautiful that he saw."

"You never mentioned him to me."

"Darren and I dated for two months, again, *before* you walked into my life. At first, I didn't know that you and I were going to be serious, and it's hardly fun, casual conversation to say... 'Oh, by the way, you know the most famous man in the area? Totally obsessed with me. So I have a restraining order against him, but he's got lots of cops in his pocket, so it's not super enforced.'" She sighed. "I thought it was over. The more I was with you, the more he appeared to fade away, and there just didn't seem to be any point in bringing him up. He was my past. Something dark and scary. You were the future."

"And you don't think I'm dark and scary?"

Did he even need to ask? Gia shook her head.

"He wanted to own everything beautiful," Oliver repeated slowly. "That means...he wanted to own you, didn't he?"

"He asked me to marry him. I said no. He went too fast with our relationship. It had only been two months, and I was already seeing alarms in all of our interactions. When I broke it off, that's when things got...rougher."

Oliver gazed tenderly at her. Tucked a lock of hair behind her ear. Nodded. "Thank you for telling me."

Uh, that was it? That was what he had to say?

"Thank you, and you understand, when he comes for you, I will be in his way."

Her stomach knotted. "Oliver—"

"I will never again watch while you die in front of me." Soft. "I will never let you feel pain when I'm close. I should have stopped this bastard long ago. I *hate* that I was gone when you needed me, but it won't happen again. I swear it. You will never be alone. You will never be scared. I will always be close when you need me."

Those words sounded so beautiful. Except for the whole her dying in front of him part. That was terrifying and creepy and a thousand other things. She had no intention of dying that night—whether in front of Oliver or anywhere else—and she certainly didn't intend for him to die, either. "You're not bulletproof."

"No, but I'm not human, either. It will take one hell of a lot more than a bullet to keep me down. Believe this, I will do whatever it takes to protect you."

She hadn't possessed enough proof to get charges pressed against Darren in the spate of break-ins and vandalisms. As for the attack at the park? She hadn't seen his face. The cops hadn't been willing to go up against him. Knowing there was no choice, she'd fled. "I want him behind bars. Locked up so he can't hurt me or anyone else. I don't want you wolfing out and killing for me."

"If he comes to kill you, he's dead."

That was chilling. "Oliver...*no*."

He curled his fingers around one of her wrists. Lifted up her hand. Pressed a kiss to her knuckles. "If I can throw him in a cell, I will. If I have to kill him in order to protect you, I will. When it comes to you, there are no limits for me. I *will not* watch you die."

"Oliver—"

He kissed her. Like a kiss was going to distract her from what was a very, very serious conversation but...

What if danger is coming? What if Darren is out there, planning an attack right now? What if this night, this moment, was all that she had with

Oliver? What if everything was already planned out and this was the night that she died?

"No!" Gia pushed against him.

Oliver took a step back.

No. This won't be it. I won't let things end this way.

"Gia?"

Her chin lifted, and she let the sheet fall. "You're not going to kiss me to distract me."

His eyes were *hot* as they traveled over her.

"I'm going to strip to distract you," she told him. "I'm going to strip, and I'm going to touch you, and I'm going to drive you crazy, and even if this is our last time together, it's going to be so amazing that it feels like we touch heaven."

"Baby, I always touch heaven with you."

How could she have forgotten the way his words would *rock* through her?

But they did. He did.

She put her hands on his bare chest. She stood on her toes, and her mouth began to kiss a hot path over him even as she felt his dick shoving toward her through the rough fabric of his jeans. The first time near the Christmas tree had been incredible. Fast and frantic and the orgasm had made her whole body quake. But this time, she wanted to touch every inch of him. To savor him.

"Get on the bed," she ordered huskily.

He did, but he pulled her with him. He ditched his jeans, sprawled on the bed, and tugged her down on top of him.

She shook her head. Positioned her body exactly where she wanted to be. Then she was wrapping her fingers around his cock and pulling it toward her mouth.

Taste. Her lips closed around him. Her tongue swirled over him. His hips flew off the bed, and Oliver's hands closed over her shoulders. "Gia!"

She kept working him. Taking more of him inside her mouth. She remembered exactly what he liked. Just how he enjoyed being stroked by her tongue. She teased and she savored, and her hands greedily touched. She was going to drive him past the point of no return—

She was flat on her back. Gia blinked. How the heck had she gotten—

"I can move fast," he told her gruffly. "Very, very fast." He licked his lips. "Two more seconds, and I would have come in your mouth."

That didn't sound like the worst plan to her.

"Instead, you'll be coming against mine." Oliver shifted his body. Spread her legs wide. Put his mouth on her. Drove his tongue *into* her. She would have flown right off the bed, but his hands clamped over her hips and held her in place as he tasted and took *his* time with her.

Licking. Sucking. Working her clit with his tongue. Then thrusting that wicked tongue into her. Over and over.

Her heels dug into the bed. She'd wanted to touch and caress all of him— "There! Yes, right there. *Oliver!*"

He licked faster.

She came, as he'd wanted, right against his mouth. Her heart thundered, and the climax had her seeing stars.

He licked her until it was done. As she struggled to catch her breath, she felt his cock press at the entrance to her body. Gia forced her languid lashes to lift.

"I love you," Oliver told her.

I never stopped loving you.

He drove into her.

Moments later, she was pretty sure they both touched paradise.

***

"So...when do I die?" They were in bed, and his arm was wrapped around her as they cuddled close. A wide yawn stretched Gia's mouth. Her body was completely replete.

"Christmas Eve. That's...that's when you died in the glimpse I saw."

She squinted at the clock. "We only have about thirty minutes until it's Christmas. Just so you know, I don't intend to leave the apartment in that thirty-minute period." She intended to stay exactly where she was. All snuggled up with Oliver.

"Good."

"If I make it through Christmas Eve, that means whatever you saw—whatever path for me, I mean—it's changed, right?" Did she sound worried? She didn't want to sound worried.

"The path for you will change no matter what." *He* sounded confident. Determined.

Her Oliver.

"We're not just going to head back to the way things were," Gia warned him. Oliver should realize this. "There will be weeks of groveling from you. Lots of hot chocolate deliveries. Random acts of awesomeness where you rub my feet for hours."

He laughed. "Consider all that done." His lips brushed her temple. "As long as I'm with you, everything is going to be okay."

Everything is going to be okay. Words she'd once tried to tell him. "The ring is in the nightstand."

She felt him stiffen. "You still have it?"

"If it's in the nightstand, I do." Silly wolf.

He jumped from the bed. Pretty much *yanked* the drawer from the nightstand. That werewolf strength was impressive, but it could also be a bit detrimental to her furniture. She'd have to caution him about that.

But he held the diamond ring with the utmost care. Completely naked, he stood by the bed, then dropped to one knee. "Gia, will you please spend the rest of your life with me?"

The rest of her life...however long it might be. "I think I already told you the answer was yes once before."

He barely seemed to be breathing.

"My answer hasn't changed," Gia said. She wiggled her fingers.

He took the hint and slid the ring into place. It gleamed so brightly, just like a brilliant star—

"Star!" It was Gia's turn to hop from the bed. She grabbed a robe and twisted it around her body. "We *cannot* go to sleep on Christmas Eve without putting the star on the tree!"

"Uh, Gia, I just asked you to marry me—"

"And I will. And it will be an awesome marriage. Lots of people will cry at the beauty of the ceremony, I'm sure, but for now..." She whirled and smiled at him. "Get those jeans on and come and help me to put the star on the tree."

"Gia..."

"It's almost Christmas," she whispered even as she felt the slight weight of the ring and wiggled her finger. "And we need the star because an angel came to you and sent *you* back to me. I want to say thank you, and I don't want to lose this second chance. The star is my thank you."

He grabbed for his jeans. "Anything to make you happy."

She rushed toward the bedroom door and swung it open. Her steps were practically flying over the floor as—

Gia stopped.

Someone was standing in front of her Christmas tree. Someone in a big, black coat. Someone who was damn well *not* Santa Claus. Someone...

Someone slowly turning toward her and revealing the gun he gripped in his hand.

"Hello, Gia," Darren Emmanuel said. "Merry Christmas."

He pulled the trigger.

CHAPTER TEN

He caught the faint scent just as the Gia opened the bedroom door. Heard the lightest creak of the floor, and claws immediately burst from Oliver's fingertips.

Someone is here. Someone who had been able to break the locks and sneak inside because Oliver had been so focused on making love to Gia. Gia had been all that he could see, smell, taste, touch...Oliver had let down his guard, and the bastard had gotten killing close.

Killing.

Oliver didn't waste time on a roar of warning. He saw the man before the tree turn, and Oliver knew he would pull up a gun. Oliver just grabbed for Gia. He lifted her up, and he tossed her toward the couch. She landed safely on the cushions.

The gun blasted. The bullet slammed into his chest.

"*Oliver!*" Gia screamed.

But he wasn't slowing down. The bullet wasn't stopping him. It hadn't hit his heart. Had instead just torn through muscle and bone and blasted out his back. A human would have been on the floor. *Good thing I'm not human.* Oliver jumped forward and ignored the strange burn that he felt in the wake of that bullet, as if his very insides had been singed. He grabbed the gun and ripped it from the bastard's hand. He threw it against the wall.

Then his hand curled around the SOB's throat. "I am going to tear you apart," he promised.

Darren Emmanuel—Oliver recognized him from freaking billboard pics and too many television ads—smiled at him. "Not if I rip you open first."

Something sank into Oliver's chest. He glanced down, thinking it was a knife, thinking the guy must've had a backup weapon on him, but, no, that wasn't a knife...

Darren had shoved his *claws* into Oliver's chest.

"Don't recognize me, do you?" Darren rasped. "But then again, the first time we met, I looked quite different." He yanked his claws out. Blood dripped from their razor-sharp edges as he swiped toward Oliver's neck. "I got you around here that night—"

Oliver caught the bastard's wrist before those claws could slice his neck. "Because of that attack, I got my *own* claws."

Darren's eyes widened. "What? No, that's not possible—"

Oliver drove his left hand—with *his* razor-sharp claws—straight into Darren's stomach. He sliced deep and hard. "Don't you know? Anything is possible."

Darren howled in pain and slammed his head toward Oliver. Oliver let him go and backed up a quick step. Oliver rubbed his palm over the bullet wound on his chest. Burned like a frigging bitch. Smoke was even rising from his skin. What was up with that?

And that was when he realized... "Silver?" He did *not* remember silver bullets being in the *glimpse* that he'd been given. *A head's up on that would have been appreciated, Cael.* "You're fucking packing silver when you're a werewolf? What kind of dumbass does that?"

Darren's breath panted out. "The kind who knows that sometimes, the best way to strike at an enemy is with a bullet and not with claws. You have to be ready for anything. I always am. I know how to disguise my scent. How to not make a sound when I approach my prey. I am the fucking apex predator."

So that explained more about why Oliver hadn't heard or scented the guy sooner. It hadn't just been because the awesome sex had distracted him so much. Good to know. But as far as the apex predator BS..."You weren't ready for me." He didn't look toward Gia. She was safe. She'd stay that way. Deliberately, he put his body between her and Darren. "Not tonight, and not the first night we met. Didn't expect *me* to be carrying silver that night, did you? But the knife was an old gift from my grandfather. Never left home without it." Now he realized that silver had saved his ass.

"Took that knife from you." Darren smiled at him and flashed teeth that were lengthening and sharpening. "Just like I'll take Gia."

"Not happening. You won't touch Gia."

"*Gia is mine!* I knew it from the first moment. She's always been meant to be mine."

"About that..." Gia coughed. "I'm not. I'm not your anything and never will be."

"You're my mate!" Darren thundered.

"Thanks, but no thanks," she returned quite clearly. "Actually, I rescind the thanks. How about just fuck off?"

Darren's face mottled with fury. His bones were snapping.

"She's not your mate," Oliver told him flatly. "A werewolf can't hurt his true mate. You do nothing but hurt her."

"Like you're any better?" Spittle flew from Darren's mouth. "Some wannabe wolf. Bet you have no power. Bet the beast controls you. Bet you rip apart every human you see."

He'd feared that. It hadn't happened. Wouldn't, not ever. "No, I just rip apart asshole werewolves who think they can terrorize the woman *I* love."

"You don't love her!" Darren slammed down on all fours.

When Darren shifted, Oliver knew he would have to do the same. He wouldn't stand a chance against the other werewolf in human form. "You don't know me." He called up his wolf. Felt it surge inside of him. Fur rippled across his skin. His bones popped and broke, and Oliver hit the floor. But first… "Gia, *go!*" She should get out of there. When the wolves battled, he didn't want to risk any harm coming to her.

"No, I think I'll stay put." Her voice was steady. Strong.

His head swung toward her. He saw that she gripped the gun in her hand.

"Loaded with silver? That's what I got from that earlier bit of chit-chat?" Gia nodded. "Excellent. Stop the shift, Darren. Stop it right now. You're going to confess to everything. I'm going to have the cops lock you away in a cell, and you won't be able to change into a wolf again and you won't be—"

"Gia!" Oliver's roar to her was more beast than anything else. It was all he could manage. Because caught half-shift, he saw that Darren was lunging for her. Darren was half-man, half-beast, all fury. All of his rage was centered on Gia. Darren shoved down with his legs and hurtled into the air. The jump would take him over Oliver and straight to Gia.

Hell, no. Oliver leapt up, too, and his claws shoved into Darren even as he heard the gun discharge.

There was a terrible scream. Blood—so much blood.

Darren fell. His body crashed onto the floor. Oliver stood over him, body heaving, and watched as Darren's half-shifted form slowly changed back into that of a man.

"He's not going to attack again." Gia's low voice.

No, he wasn't. Darren's heart wasn't beating. *Because my claws stopped it.*

Oliver's body began to ease back into fully human form.

In the distance, he could hear a siren. Gia's neighbors had probably called the cops when they heard the first gunshot blast.

"Did I kill him?" she asked.

The bullet had hit barely a breath before Oliver's claws had cut into Darren's heart.

Oliver caught her hand. He had blood on his fingers. But not her blood. Not this time. "I did it. When the cops ask, I did it all. He broke into your apartment. He tried to kill you. I stopped him."

But she shook her head. "You're not lying for me."

"Gia…" They'd been over this. He would do *anything* for—

"We tell them the truth."

"The truth is that he was a freaking werewolf and so am I."

"Maybe not that truth," she allowed. She bent and put her fingers to Darren's throat. "Just making sure."

There was no need for that. Oliver already was sure.

"He broke in. We had to defend ourselves," Gia said as she stared at Darren's body. "We'll tell the cops as much of the truth as we can."

As much as they could, without getting tossed into a padded cell. *They won't believe Darren was a werewolf. And if I show them what I am, I'll get locked away while the world freaks out.*

The cops were going to ask questions about the guy's wounds. Not like those wounds were gonna match up with any knife. Dammit, this night was gonna be tough. Before it was over, Oliver might very well be in a cage.

He wrapped his fingers around her shoulders. Pulled her close. "All that matters is that you're okay."

He heard the rush of footsteps in the hall. The cops were definitely there. Oliver inhaled deeply, then slowly walked for the door. Gia was at his side.

He opened the door. Saw two cops waiting. They really had made some pretty fast time. He wondered which neighbor had called for them—

"Cael said you'd need some backup tonight," the cop on the right said. "Alpha, what can we do?"

Alpha? Wait, what?

"I'm Officer Bridgette Black, and this is my partner, Evan Gerard. We're here to help."

"Heard there's a rogue wolf in there," Evan said as his nostrils flared. "We don't take kindly to predatory werewolves in Mistletoe Falls." He flashed a little fang.

Oliver rocked back on his heels. *They are both werewolves.* "He's dead. He broke in, and he was attacking Gia." The truth. She'd wanted him to tell it. He was. "He lunged at her, and she fired a gun. *His* gun. He brought it here so he could kill her with it."

The cop who'd flashed fang shot her a sympathetic look. "Sorry, ma'am. We're not all monsters."

No, they weren't.

"She fired at him, and I slashed up at him with my claws. I aimed for his heart." Simple. Brutal. "He was dead before he hit the floor." With each word Oliver spoke, a weight seemed to lift from him. "He's got claw marks on him. Not like those will match up with a normal weapon when an ME examines him."

"Don't worry about that," Bridgette assured him. "Our ME knows the score." She assessed him. "Those wounds of yours healing okay?"

He barely felt them. "I'm fine."

"He's not fine," Gia announced. "He needs a doctor."

"My wounds heal on their own, baby," he told her quietly. "They'll be totally gone in about five minutes." If he'd shifted fully, they would have already been mended. The claw marks on Darren hadn't healed because he'd died before they could. They'd remained on him in death.

Gia frowned up at him. The little furrow appeared between her brows. *God, I missed that furrow.*

Gia looked back at the cops. "What exactly does it mean to say that he's alpha?"

"Well..." Bridgette put her hand on her holster. "He'll probably be elected mayor in the next election."

Oliver's temples began to pound.

"The alpha is the strongest wolf in the area. No one can take him down. No one can break him." Bridgette cleared her throat. "But if you two don't mind, we really need to secure this scene."

Oh. Right. They backed up so the cops could come inside.

"I don't think they're going to be hauling either one of us to jail," Gia whispered.

He knew the cops probably heard her. "No."

"You really going to be mayor?" Gia wanted to know.

He had no freaking clue. That didn't matter, though. She mattered. His hands swept over her as he searched for any wounds. There were none. This time, she hadn't been the one to bleed out and die.

Darren had died. He wouldn't be hurting her ever again.

Chapter Eleven

She should probably be in shock. Gia figured she should be crying or shuddering or having some sort of breakdown as she stood in the snow outside of her apartment and watched the body of Darren Emmanuel get wheeled outside. Snow fell on her, and it *was* cold, but she didn't so much as quiver.

Her nightmare was over. In those last terrible moments, she'd seen her own death staring back at her from Darren's glowing eyes. She hadn't wanted to shoot. But she *had* wanted to keep living. She'd wanted to have a life with Oliver. To have a home and a family and a chance to be happy once more.

Dying because of Darren's twisted obsession hadn't been on her agenda.

"Here, Gia. Take my coat." She turned at the voice. She hadn't even heard someone approach, but there was a blond man, a few inches shorter than her own height, standing beside her. He held a white coat out to her.

"Oh, no, I couldn't." She shook her head. "It's cold. You need it. I'll be going back inside soon."

He smiled at her. "You didn't have to let him in, you know."

"Excuse me?"

"When he knocked at your door, you could have slammed that door shut on Oliver. He'd hurt you. You didn't have to let him back into your heart."

Goosebumps rose, but they had nothing to do with the cold. "Who are you?"

"Cael."

Cael. "You...sent the cops to us?"

A nod. "Thought you could use someone who understood." He hummed. Then he just...dropped onto the ground.

She frowned down at him. "What are you doing?"

"Making a snow angel. Bet you did that as a child, didn't you? Got in the snow, spread your arms, and made beautiful wings."

A man had died that night. He was being loaded into the back of some kind of coroner's van or something. Making wings didn't seem like the wisest choice at the moment, but she didn't tell him that. The last thing she wanted to do was hurt his feelings.

"I always wanted wings. Waited and waited for them..." His tongue poked through his lips as he moved his arms rapidly. "Sometimes, you need a bit of patience." He jumped to his feet. Snow fell off him. "What do you think?"

She looked at the misshapen angel, then back at his beaming face. "It's beautiful."

He touched her shoulder. "You have a kind heart."

Not always, she didn't.

"You didn't have to answer the door," he said again. "When Oliver came knocking, you could have ignored him. But you let him in. He'd hurt you, but you were willing to try to forgive him." He searched her gaze. "Why?"

"Because I love him."

"That's a good answer." But he'd lost his smile. "I'm really glad you opened the door. I can help push, but I can't control. No one can control what others do."

There was something about him that nagged at her. "We've met before."

He turned away. "Have we?"

"I..." Gia struggled to remember. "When I first came to town, didn't I see you at the gas station? Weren't you the one who told me that this was a nice town to call home?" The memory was there, teasing her. A half-forgotten conversation at a gas pump. She'd thought he was just being friendly. She'd been tired and distracted. But...

He whistled. "It *is* a nice town, isn't it?"

It had been him at the gas station.

"You have a good night, Gia. Maybe you can get around to putting up that star."

Her mouth dropped open. The snow seemed to thicken and a flurry of flakes hit her.

"Gia?" Oliver brushed against her. "Baby, you don't have a coat." He shouldered out of his. Put it around her and wrapped her in his arms. "I know tonight was hard, terrifying, but we can go forward from here. You're safe now. The cops are working to help you. They've got lots of evidence on Darren. Turns out, another woman had been stalked by him, too. They're putting more pieces together, but the important thing is that you're protected. He won't hurt you or anyone else again, and—"

She was struggling to see through the snow. Craning her neck.

"Gia?"

She licked her lips. Tasted the snowflakes. "Is there a snow angel on the ground beside me?"

"Uh, yes."

Right. "And your guardian angel is named Cael?"

"Yes."

"The same Cael the cops mentioned?"

"I would imagine so. Probably only one Cael running around town getting into all the paranormal business."

She fell back against him.

"Sweetheart?"

"I think your angel just visited me."

"He's actually not quite an angel, not yet. He didn't have his wings."

She looked down at the snow. At that beautiful angel. "Something tells me he's going to get them."

***

They went to the rundown bar. It was long after midnight. Christmas had come. The town was quiet, everyone sleeping, and the door of the bar? Unlocked.

It was empty inside. Oliver stared in wonder because it looked as if the place had been abandoned for years. No furniture. Just dust. No alcohol lining the shelves behind the bar. Instead, they were empty. The place was cold and dark, and Gia was using the light from her phone to shine it around the interior. Oliver could see perfectly in the dark, but he knew she needed that bit of illumination.

"He was here," Oliver assured her. "He was trying whiskey. Chugging it down and coughing up a lung when he swallowed too much." He walked to the bar. Put his hands on the old, scarred surface. "He wanted me to make a wish."

Gia's light danced over the empty shelves once more. "I believe you."

She always had. She'd believed *in* him.

He turned back to her.

"But he's not here now." She looked up, tilting her head back as she gazed at the ceiling. "Maybe he went home. It is Christmas, after all."

Yes. It was.

"I...I don't want to go back to my place tonight." She lowered her voice. "If it's okay with you, could I spend the night—"

"Yes." She didn't need to finish her sentence. "Always, *yes*. And guess what? I even have a tree because you see, I fell in love with this amazing lady once. I met her at a tree lot, and she *loved* Christmas. So when the holiday season came around, I had to put up the tree because...because she would have wanted me to do that. Because having the tree reminded me of her." He brushed a kiss over her lips. "Because maybe some miracle would happen, and I'd see her, and if she came to my home, I wanted it to be ready for her." Even if the rest of the house was cold and stark, he'd needed the tree for *her*.

Her hand rose to caress his cheek. "You're all I want for Christmas."

"And you're my wish." It was the truth. He cleared his throat. "You hear that, Cael? You gave me my Christmas wish. A second chance at life with Gia. You did that. So thank you."

The words seemed to echo around him.

But there was no response. No Cael.

He was probably long gone.

Oliver's fingers wrapped with Gia's, and they headed for the door. She pulled it open, and a happy, light peal sounded as the bell above the door rang.

It *hadn't* jingled when they'd entered the bar.

But it was clear and beautiful right then.

A wide smile split his face. "Gia, do you know what is supposed to happen when a bell rings?"

She laughed. "I'm pretty sure something magical happens to an angel or, rather, to an angel intern."

"Yeah, it does." He had to kiss her once more. "And something magical happens to a werewolf, too."

"Oh, really? What?"

"A werewolf gets his wish." His wish was right by his side. He would cherish her, protect her, and love her...forever.

Merry Christmas, Cael, and thank you.

THE END

A Note from The Author

Thank you for reading IT'S A WONDERUL WEREWOLF! I hope that you enjoyed the story. This is my absolute favorite time of the year, and I was so excited to write this novella.

A few years ago, I released A VAMPIRE'S CHRISTMAS CAROL, and, ever since then, I had wanted to write a Christmas romance that featured a werewolf hero. IT'S A WONDERFUL WEREWOLF was my chance to finally achieve that goal!

If you'd like to stay updated on my releases and sales, please join my newsletter list.

https://cynthiaeden.com/newsletter/

Again, thank you for reading IT'S A WONDERUL WEREWOLF.

Best,
Cynthia Eden
cynthiaeden.com

ABOUT THE AUTHOR

Cynthia Eden is a *New York Times*, *USA Today*, *Digital Book World*, and *IndieReader* best-seller.

Cynthia writes sexy tales of contemporary romance, romantic suspense, and paranormal romance. Since she began writing full-time in 2005, Cynthia has written over one hundred novels and novellas.

Cynthia lives along the Alabama Gulf Coast. She loves romance novels, horror movies, and chocolate.

For More Information

- *cynthiaeden.com*
- *facebook.com/cynthiaedenfanpage*

HER OTHER WORKS

Holiday Romances

- Deck The Halls
- One Hot Holiday
- Midnight Bite
- Christmas With A Spy
- A Vampire's Christmas Carol

Trouble For Hire

- No Escape From War (Book 1)
- Don't Play With Odin (Book 2)
- Jinx, You're It (Book 3)
- Remember Ramsey (Book 4)

Death and Moonlight Mystery

- Step Into My Web (Book 1)
- Save Me From The Dark (Book 2)

Wilde Ways

- Protecting Piper (Book 1)
- Guarding Gwen (Book 2)
- Before Ben (Book 3)
- The Heart You Break (Book 4)
- Fighting For Her (Book 5)
- Ghost Of A Chance (Book 6)
- Crossing The Line (Book 7)

- Counting On Cole (Book 8)
- Chase After Me (Book 9)
- Say I Do (Book 10)
- Roman Will Fall (Book 11)
- The One Who Got Away (Book 12)
- Pretend You Want Me (Book 13)

Dark Sins

- Don't Trust A Killer (Book 1)
- Don't Love A Liar (Book 2)

Lazarus Rising

- Never Let Go (Book One)
- Keep Me Close (Book Two)
- Stay With Me (Book Three)
- Run To Me (Book Four)
- Lie Close To Me (Book Five)
- Hold On Tight (Book Six)
- Lazarus Rising Volume One (Books 1 to 3)
- Lazarus Rising Volume Two (Books 4 to 6)

Dark Obsession Series

- Watch Me (Book 1)
- Want Me (Book 2)
- Need Me (Book 3)
- Beware Of Me (Book 4)
- Only For Me (Books 1 to 4)

Mine Series

- Mine To Take (Book 1)
- Mine To Keep (Book 2)
- Mine To Hold (Book 3)

- Mine To Crave (Book 4)
- Mine To Have (Book 5)
- Mine To Protect (Book 6)
- Mine Box Set Volume 1 (Books 1-3)
- Mine Box Set Volume 2 (Books 4-6)

Bad Things

- The Devil In Disguise (Book 1)
- On The Prowl (Book 2)
- Undead Or Alive (Book 3)
- Broken Angel (Book 4)
- Heart Of Stone (Book 5)
- Tempted By Fate (Book 6)
- Wicked And Wild (Book 7)
- Saint Or Sinner (Book 8)
- Bad Things Volume One (Books 1 to 3)
- Bad Things Volume Two (Books 4 to 6)
- Bad Things Deluxe Box Set (Books 1 to 6)

Bite Series

- Forbidden Bite (Bite Book 1)
- Mating Bite (Bite Book 2)

Blood and Moonlight Series

- Bite The Dust (Book 1)
- Better Off Undead (Book 2)
- Bitter Blood (Book 3)
- Blood and Moonlight (The Complete Series)

Purgatory Series

- The Wolf Within (Book 1)
- Marked By The Vampire (Book 2)

- Charming The Beast (Book 3)
- Deal with the Devil (Book 4)
- The Beasts Inside (Books 1 to 4)

Bound Series

- Bound By Blood (Book 1)
- Bound In Darkness (Book 2)
- Bound In Sin (Book 3)
- Bound By The Night (Book 4)
- Bound in Death (Book 5)
- Forever Bound (Books 1 to 4)

Stand-Alone Romantic Suspense

- Never Gonna Happen
- One Hot Holiday
- Secret Admirer
- First Taste of Darkness
- Sinful Secrets
- Until Death
- Christmas With A Spy